To my husband, my compass.

www.mascotbooks.com

Ruby Foo and the Traveling Kitchen: Ruby Goes to Spain

For more information, please contact:
Mascot Books
620 Herndon Parkway, Suite 320
Herndon, VA 20170
info@mascotbooks.com

Library of Congress Control Number: 2020923199

CPSIA Code: PRFRE0121A
ISBN-13: 978-1-64543-635-5

Printed in Canada

RUBY FOO
AND THE TRAVELING KITCHEN

My Journal
Tapas
W Ruby Foo

KEEP
CALM
AND
COOK
ON

Adventure #2: Ruby Goes to Spain

Tiffany Foo

Illustrated by Chiara Savarese

Chapter 1

Functional or Fashionable Packing

Isabel softly kicked around her soccer ball, watching me sit silently, flanked by piles of clothes on my floor and complaining under my breath. School would be out in less than a week, but since we were leaving for our trip to Spain right afterward, I was trying to pack early. We had already been battling my clothes for several days, and my turquoise-painted walls were closing in on us. Isabel was tired and irritable, and I was downright fried.

"How far did you get?" my best friend asked, dribbling the soccer ball expertly on her knee. "I've got to get home pretty soon and work on my extra credit."

I nodded absentmindedly. Our history teacher, Mrs. Zecker, had given almost everyone else in my class Bs on their final assignments. No one else had found a story in their family quite as personal as mine, so I received a

B+. Since Mrs. Zecker is also our National Junior Honor Society team leader, she's given everyone the opportunity to do more research and see if they can find out more. Mrs. Zecker told us we could all email her our updates if we found anything else over the summer, but Isabel was trying to get hers finished before our trip so we could just focus on having fun and finding new foods in Spain!

I sighed eyeing the clock. "Well, so far I have mostly ruled these piles out." I gestured to three mountains of clothes, watching as Isabel rolled her eyes at the other half dozen piles left in the running. "Hopefully I don't need my ski sweater, too." I made a fist and knocked on my wooden bedpost. "Get it? Ski sweater—because of all the mountains of clothes?"

Isabel laughed. "I think you need to take the advice you give to Ryan: if you have to explain the joke, then it isn't funny. You are so superstitious sometimes. I don't know why you need to knock on wood over a sweater."

"Ugh, Isabel, you sound like my mom! I need to knock on wood as a 'just in case.' Like, just in case I lose a sweater during vacation, I should bring more." I turned to one of the "maybe" piles on the floor. "Speaking of my mom . . . she can't see my room like this; it irks her to see "piles" of anything. I don't think I can use my usual strategy and hide the view from the doorway."

Isabel chimed in, "Well, let's get rid of the piles right

now! My mom told me it can get really, really hot in July in Madrid. Honestly, I don't think it's a good idea to bring all those sweaters. I didn't want to hurt your feelings, but you need to get rid of most of those clothes."

I stared longingly at my sweater and sweatshirt pile. "But I get cold sometimes, and I love comfy clothes. Plus, those are summer sweaters and sweatshirts. I know your parents have everything planned. Those links you've sent me about Madrid and food markets—I can't wait to go. Maybe long sleeves would impede my ability to eat?"

Isabel nodded. "It will definitely hamper your ability to get your foodie going. Three sweaters are too much."

"Let me get this straight, Isabel—you think *three* sweaters is excessive?"

Just at that moment, Isabel lost control of the soccer ball. Even without any force behind it, when it softly tapped one of my larger mountains, the whole thing avalanched.

"Isabel! Stop playing ball in my room!"

Isabel raised an eyebrow at me. I instantly heard myself, and we both started to laugh.

"Ugh! We are both starting to sound like our mothers, so we must be hangry. It is clearly time for a snack; maybe that will help us with our homework and packing—we just need some vitamins."

3

Isabel smiled. "Great idea! I am definitely on the verge of hangry!"

We both laughed and said simultaneously, "Dessert dumplings!"

Yes, we were best friends for a reason—we both have the same great ideas!

We sped downstairs and started getting out the ingredients for dessert dumplings. I noticed Isabel taking out the marshmallows.

"What are those for?"

"I thought we'd do the s'more dumplings?"

"Oh, I thought we were making the lemon Nutella dumplings. I guess we could do both, but we don't have a lot of time—my mom will be home soon, and she will flip out if I'm not done packing."

"Right, I know," said Isabel. "Let's race—everything has to be done in under thirty minutes, just like on the cooking shows, like *Sliced Junior*. I will make the s'more dumplings, and you make the lemon Nutella!"

"Great idea again! Ready to compete? Let's see who can get the most Nutella into their dumplings. If your chocolate bursts through, you're *sliced*, no matter how it tastes!"

5

S'more Dessert Dumpling

Total: 45 minutes–1 hour   Prep: 20–25 minutes
Cook: 20-30 minutes   Yield: 4 servings

Ingredients

✓ Chocolate chips

✓ Mini marshmallows

✓ Graham crackers (crushed)

✓ Jumbo dumpling wrappers (18–20)

✓ Canola or peanut oil

Directions

1. Place 1 dumpling wrapper in the palm of your hand.
2. Fill or add to dumpling wrapper with 3 or 4 chocolate chips.
3. Fill or add to dumpling wrapper with 3 or 4 mini marshmallows.
4. Fill or add 1 teaspoon of crushed graham cracker crumbs.
5. Gently dampen the edges of the dumpling wrapper with water.
6. Fold all dumpling wrapper points or edges to the middle and pinch together (the shape should look like a little envelope).
7. Heat 3–4 tablespoons of oil in a frying pan.
8. Gently place your dumplings in the heated pan.
9. Add other dumplings to pan. Space dumplings about 1–2 inches apart in pan.
10. Once the dumplings are a light golden brown on one side, gently turn them and pan fry the other side until lightly golden brown.
11. Remove from pan and place on a cooling rack for 5–10 minutes.

★ Optional: Use mini deep fryer. Set at 350 degrees. Place 2–3 dumplings in deep fryer for 1–2 minutes.

6

Nutella & Lemon Dessert Dumpling

Total: 45 minutes–1 hour   Prep: 20–25 minutes
Cook: 20-30 minutes   Yield: 4 servings

Ingredients

✓ Nutella or any hazelnut/chocolate spread

✓ Meyer lemon curd or any jarred lemon curd

✓ Jumbo dumpling wrappers

✓ Canola or peanut oil

Directions

1. Place 1 dumpling wrapper in the palm of your hand.
2. Fill with ½–¾ of a teaspoon of the Nutella.
3. Fill with ½–¾ of a teaspoon of meyer lemon curd.
4. Gently dampen the edges of the dumpling wrapper with water.
5. Fold all dumpling wrapper points or edges to the middle and pinch together. (The shape should look like a little envelope).
6. Heat 3–4 tablespoons of oil in a frying pan.
7. Gently place your dumplings in the heated pan.
8. Add in other dumplings to pan. Space dumplings about 1–2 inches apart in pan.
9. Once the dumplings are a light golden brown on one side, gently turn them and pan fry the other side until lightly golden brown.
10. Remove from pan and place on a cooling rack for 5–10 minutes.

★ Plate both dumplings followed by Dessert Judging!
★ Optional: Use mini deep fryer. Set at 350 degrees. Place 2–3 dumplings in deep fryer for 1–2 minutes.

7

As we both slid the last of our dumplings from the cooking oil and onto the cooling racks, I looked around the kitchen and realized that the speed of our competition had not necessarily made clean-up easier or faster.

"Well, now we've got to get my bedroom *and* this kitchen in order before Mom comes home!"

My brothers came rumbling up the stairs from the basement. "We smell cookies! Where are the cookies?"

I pointed to the kitchen as they charged past us.

"Those aren't cookies!"

"I know," I shouted as Isabel and I ran into the kitchen to stop the dumplings from vanishing. "You two can take part in our *Sliced* competition. These are dumplings; take one from plate A and one from plate B, and then tell us which one you vote for."

"Wait!" shouted Isabel. "Don't skew the vote, they need a sprinkle of powdered sugar!"

"Okay, Isabel, don't get so competitive; make sure you powder both plates, or they will know which one yours is."

"Now who's getting competitive?" Isabel said as she rolled her eyes.

I shot her a face and rolled my eyes right back.

Isabel laughed. "Calm down, Ruby. You are the queen of eye-rolling."

"Ruby isn't the queen of eye-rolling. I am the king!" Ryan shouted, pulling all four-foot-ten of himself up tall to demonstrate his technique.

Nic scoffed. "Nice try, minion."

Ryan looked disappointed for a moment. Ever since his birthday, he'd been trying to find something he could beat both Nic and me at, and it was way past old already. You could almost see him cross another item off the long list in his head.

"How long do we have to wait to eat one of these dumplings? I can tell you right now, it doesn't matter who made which, because you are both sliced. Plate A looks slightly burned, and Plate B is empty," Ryan declared.

I looked up to see Nic shielding his mouth with his hand, blocking the view of the only part of his face that his thick, long bangs didn't cover. His other hand cupped however many of my dumplings he hadn't already been able to cram in his mouth.

"Nic! You took all of my Nutella and lemon dumplings!"

Nic shrugged his shoulders. "Chill. All of you need to chill. I obviously cast my vote for lemon. You know lemon is always the best."

With that, he disappeared back into the basement.

My mouth gaping, I turned to Isabel and said, "Now

9

what?"

She replied, "I guess nothing. Literally nothing. Both plates are empty!"

I turned around to see Ryan running away with plate A. He yelled out, "I don't like lemon anyway."

Isabel and I both sighed and walked back to the deck to finish what was left of our dumplings, grateful we'd managed to hide a few away before my brothers had gotten to them. I'd just bitten into my first Nutella and lemon dumpling when I heard the garage door open and realized Mom was home—and about to walk into a big mess in the kitchen and an even bigger mess in my bedroom.

I groaned, counting down the seconds before I had to deal with a very angry mom or one of my irritating brothers again. "I can't wait to just get away from my family for a little while!"

"Wait, did your mom really not tell you?" Isabel mumbled, trying to chew through a huge mouthful of dumpling.

"Tell me what?"

"My mom . . . she invited . . . your whole family."

My jaw dropped. "What? When? How? Why?"

Just then, my mother came around the corner, looking as unpleased as I felt.

RUBY FOO

Chapter 2

Mission: Madrid

Mom spun right into a parking spot far and away from the car congestion. Anyone who shops at the mall or Target knows that Saturdays are the busiest days. We were ready to brave the crowds and shopping cart bottlenecks because, after my mom went through my piles, the things we still needed formed a pretty short list: a new backpack and travel skorts. She was optimistic that we could be in and out like this was a drive-through. I had not been optimistic about much since I'd learned my trip to Spain was a full-fledged "family adventure."

Isabel tagged along, chirping away with Mom as I sulked. "It is really hot in Spain in July. Plus, there may or may not be air-conditioning, and many tourist spots require pants and skirts, especially the churches."

I was struggling to stay mad. We'd been so hyped for our

11

big adventure, and a big part of me still was. Plus, my mom and I love shopping together. It was hard to keep pouting when Mom and Isabel officially labeled our shopping spree "Mission: Madrid."

The Fantastic Foo's shopping target? A skort—with cell phone pockets. We needed to dress in a conservative, yet travel-savvy way. My tennis skort was too short for touring in an old European country, and it seemed like not a single summer clothing item I owned had pockets.

My mom shouted to me from across the aisles of people, "Guess what, Ruby? I learned there are provinces in Spain, just like in China. We should look up how many provinces there are in Spain compared to China . . . wouldn't that be fun?"

I turned, shaking my head in disbelief that she was trying to hold a conversation while we were shopping. And, she was actually telling me to research provinces! Under my breath, I said, "I am sure I will learn all about it once I get there. I don't think we need to do that now."

My mom gave me a slight disapproving glare, as if she'd heard me.

I sighed, rolled my eyes, and whipped out my phone, tapping through quickly. "Okay. Based on some random website, there are twenty-three Chinese provinces and fifty Spanish provinces, despite the fact that China has nearly a billion more people in it than Spain. You could fit almost nineteen Spains inside of China, landmass-wise. Obviously, this requires more research than I am willing to pursue."

Mom pursed her lips, clearly unhappy that I was unhappy. She motioned with her arm that she had found something, and I closed the gap between us.

"All I know, Ruby, is that Spain requires that we dress appropriately and respectfully when we tour and visit with elders, just like the Chinese culture," she said, handing me a longer skort to try on.

"You knew all the way back at the post office, didn't you?" I accused her, not letting her change the subject.

My entire family had visited the post office for my passport appointment several weeks ago. I had been trying not to talk about Madrid because I still could not believe I was going abroad! I hadn't wanted to jinx anything—since the moment Mrs. García had invited me along on the trip, it'd seemed like a dream. Officially renewing my passport made it finally feel real to me.

Unfortunately, all Ryan and Nic did was joke about everyone's passport photo.

"You look like a thief, Nic!"

"Well, you look like you are in second grade."

I hadn't understood why my brothers were there, too,

especially since they'd just goofed off and irritated everyone in line. My mom had explained that since I was a minor, both she and my dad needed to be present for me to renew my passport; since they'd needed to take off work and coordinate to make that happen, they'd thought it best to renew everyone's at the same time. It had seemed believable enough at the time, but now . . .

Mom sighed. "Isabel's little brother, Nino, asked if Ryan could go, so Mrs. García had the great idea to invite Nic, too, since Guille is only a year older and they are both taking Spanish in school. It took some time to solidify all the details, Ruby, and I wasn't positive it was all going to work out until recently. I didn't want to get anyone's hopes up until I knew for certain," she said before trying to change the subject again. "I've never heard the name 'Guille' before!"

"Ugh, Mom. His given name is Guillermo, which is William in English. Don't try to distract me. I am still salty about traveling with Nic and Ryan. It's tough enough just fighting over video games in our basement," I said.

"The Spanish nickname, our version of 'Will,' is Guille, just like we call Antonio 'Nino,'" Isabel volunteered, trying to steer the conversation away from my anger.

It wasn't working. Thinking about all the times my brothers had irritated me just this week so far, I cried,

"Mom, why? Why are you letting Ryan and Nic go with me to Spain? That is so unfair! I thought this was my vacation with my friend!"

Isabel suddenly got very interested in a rack of clothing a little way away. She looked as embarrassed as I felt about my outburst. I knew I was being a brat, but I really was upset.

My mom was silent until Isabel moved out of earshot, then laid into me in a cool, calm voice: "You listen here, young lady. Mrs. García invited you on this very special trip for you and your friend Isabel. Mrs. García also invited Ryan and Nic for a very special trip with Antonio and Guillermo. Don't be self-absorbed and let their invitation diminish your special invitation and time abroad. I can tell you right now, if you do not get yourself in check, you won't be traveling anywhere this summer."

I felt my eyes well up with tears and nodded.

My mom hugged me tightly. "I love you, Ruby. Who is my big girl?"

I smiled through my tears and hugged her back. "I am. I'm sorry."

Mom smiled, relieved. "You never know—you may have fun with your brothers tagging along. Try to think of it as an adventure for all of you. Your dad and I can only join you for a few days, so it's your job to find the best food we absolutely need to eat and the best places that we absolutely have to visit before we get there, okay? Plus, Isabel will need you . . ."

I found that last part odd, but I just made a mental note to ask her what she meant later. I nodded, wiping away my tears, and activated my Fantastic Foo powers. I had a job to do, and "Mission: Madrid" was just getting started.

We bought two skorts of "appropriate" length for touring, but nothing we found had pockets for cell phones. Of course, as usual, all the boys' stuff had pockets galore.

"Don't worry. We'll sew our own pockets into one of your jackets," my mom said as we packed up the car and headed home. "You can tie the jacket around your waist since you always get cold—that way you always have a set of pockets and you're prepped! Great idea?"

The moment we walked in the door, Isabel and I watched in amazement as my mom took one of Ryan's old sports shirts, cut a large rectangle, and sewed it into my sports jacket.

"Here! Or should I say *aquí*?" Mom said proudly, holding up my new travel jacket.

We were impressed, to say the least. Mom had a little of her own superpower, obviously. Isabel declared that we should turn sewing pockets for girls' clothes into our business. It makes sense: girls are always the ones with stuff like phones, lip balm, and hair clips to cart around. We started posting pockets on our Pinterest page, and Isabel and I brainstormed what we could call our business on Etsy. Of course, my mom, always the innovator, suggested we start our own clothing line with all the pocketed clothes we wanted—but after we return from Spain.

"Don't get distracted from 'Mission: Madrid!' Make the most of your trip—'when in Rome . . .'" Mom said.

Isabel and I giggled, excited again for our trip. I am not sure what that phrase means. I need to search for that online because I haven't been to Rome—yet.

★ ★ ★

Before Isabel left to work on her extra credit and pack her own luggage, she reminded me, "Don't forget, my abuela learned a lot of English from watching television. My abuela speaks Spanish, Italian, and English! She suggested that we watch Spanish movies without any subtitles."

Finally packed since I didn't have anything yet to add to my own NJHS extra credit, I settled down on my couch and searched for the Spanish channels. I came across the Narnia and Harry Potter movies in Spanish; I scheduled

17

both for recording so I could pause and jump back to catch any words I didn't understand.

Just as I started watching, Nic materialized out of nowhere and sat down beside me.

"What are you doing?" he said, taking one earbud out of his ear to actually grace me with his presence.

"Isabel's abuela said we should watch movies in Spanish so we at least can pick up some of the words when we visit."

"Hmm. I guess. What did you find?"

I put on the ending of *Narnia* in Spanish.

"What's an 'aboo-lea?'" said Ryan.

I had no idea where he'd come from, but he sat quietly, seriously playing his video game. He is such a little imp; mischievous and adorable all in one, especially now, with his chin buried in his chest, accentuating his baby cheeks.

Eyes glued to his screen, he repeated, "Well, Ruby, what's an 'aboo-lea?'"

I laughed. "It means 'grandma' in Spanish, just like PoPo means 'grandma' in Chinese. It's pronounced *ahbweh-la*."

Nic chimed in, "The a at the end is feminine. If there is an o, then it's masculine. So, *ahbweh-lo* for grandpa. That's what my Spanish teacher told us."

Without making eye contact, Ryan responded, "*Qué?* That's all I know. Oh, and I know *stupid-o.*"

Nic shook his head and put his earbuds back in. Of course, I had to tell him to lower his music because I couldn't hear anything. "How can you expect to speak Spanish if you aren't going to listen to the movie?"

He smirked. "I will always be one step ahead of you, Ruby. I am listening to Spanish music. It is this new artist I found, the song is 'Contigo.'"

He passed me an earbud. Surprisingly, I liked it. "Wow. Can you send that to me?"

"You are so technologically awkward, Ruby. You don't send songs. Just go to your music account and add it to your playlist," Nic said, brushing his peppercorn-colored mane up out of his eyes. "See, that's just another example of how I'm smarter than you." He nodded as if we were in agreement, got up, and walked away.

He has this lanky gait now that he is so tall. It's lanky, but not awkward—it's like a confident, sly teen boy thing. Girls definitely didn't have it yet.

I continued to scroll through the recorded movies and murmured to myself, "One day, I will beat him. He thinks he's so clever."

I'd forgotten Ryan was in the room until he said quietly,

"I will beat both of you one day. I may be little now, but everyone knows that the youngest ends up being the best."

I took a deep breath and wondered if any of us would survive this trip.

Chapter 3

Eager for España

Finally, school was finished, and the big day had arrived. We crushed all our carefully packed luggage in the overhead bins, and all our backpacks were stuffed under the seats. I was worried I wouldn't have easy access to my tablet and that my protective cover wasn't as protective as all the reviews had promised. It was bright red so I wouldn't get it mixed up with my brother's. *Ugh.* I wondered what we must look like to other passengers—spoiled little American kids with their tech. But in our defense, most schools required this technology; plus, I was using mine for education: reading, cooking, and pinning books and recipes. Since Isabel hadn't gotten enough information for her extra credit assignment on her family history, I knew she was busy using hers to work on actual schoolwork on the plane—even in the middle of the summer!

Four across didn't leave much space for Isabel and me to talk about girl stuff, since we were flanked by Nic and Mrs. García. We were slightly miserable, packed together like tightly rolled enchiladas in a baking dish for the next eight hours. Meanwhile, Mr. García was sitting a row behind, rooted in his chair and pounding away at his laptop while Nino and Ryan played video games together next to him. Guille fell asleep before takeoff.

Isabel kept trying to ask her mom for any Spanish family history, but Mrs. García was fidgety and distracted. She looked exhausted already, and soon after we took off, she leaned over to Nic and kindly requested that he reach for her inflatable neck pillow and blanket. Nic retrieved it and unfolded it for her.

I gave him the evil eye. "As if you would ever do that for me!"

Nic slyly shrugged his shoulders. "What can I say? Always the gentleman." He placed his earbuds in, fixed his neck pillow, and fell asleep almost immediately.

Mrs. García whispered, "Issy, why don't you research some recipes you would like the tías to cook with both of you?"

Isabel pulled out her tablet. "I have a list, but believe it or not, Mom, you cook most of this at home. I guess I'm lucky, but I really wanted something authentic."

23

Mrs. García smiled. "My cooking is authentic, Izzy! But everyone has their way. We will be spending more time with Tía Lorena. You can ask her for her recipe ideas. I am sure the tías have more traditional recipes that will be 'ancestral amazing.'"

Her eyes lit up as if she had just coined the perfect catchphrase. It was extra. Isabel and I acknowledged this fact, rolling our eyes and smirking.

"Mom, you are so extra. Hey, why are we spending more time with Tía Lorena?"

"Thanks! Oh—uh, I don't know. I guess . . . I thought it would be nice to spend some more time with my favorite tía—you know, maybe just the girls. You'll get a real Spaniard's perspective. Ancestral amazing!"

Ugh, she said it again. I whispered to Isabel, "Maybe you should tell her that 'extra' isn't a compliment."

We both snickered, and Isabel replied, "No way. I am not telling her anything. I wonder what she meant by 'just the girls?'"

For some reason I thought back to our shopping trip and kicked myself for never asking Mom what she'd meant when she'd said Isabel would need me. I shook off the feeling that the trip was related to her odd comment and joked, "I hope it isn't some Spanish STEM class!"

24

Isabel gasped. "Oh no! Some lady named Ms. Martinez has been calling my mom a *lot*! What if she is a Spanish tutor for STEM?!"

We glanced suspiciously at Mrs. García. Knowing both our moms, it was totally believable that they would have secretly enrolled us in some summer science/technology/engineering/math class.

"Maybe Tía Lorena can help me find some more family history for my extra credit, though. I tried asking Mom if there were any more personal stories from around World War II, but she was super distracted and busy getting ready for the trip," Isabel said as we turned back to our Spanish recipe wish list.

By the time Isabel and I finished revising, it was too late to watch a movie because the flight attendant's announcements in three different languages kept interrupting us. So, we closed our eyes and turned our heads since Ryan and Nino wouldn't turn their lights off and they kept checking the flight path. I could barely move, as Nic was asleep headfirst over his snack tray.

★ ★ ★

As soon as the airplane doors opened, I felt ready to pounce. We followed the signs that said *aduanas* (customs) and after passing through without a hitch, followed the *salida* signs to exit.

The airport doors opened, and we watched as the flurry of motorcycles, mini cars, and taxi cabs that populated the streets sped past, weaving between the roundabouts that surrounded old architecture in the many central plazas.

Mrs. García said, "This is Madrid! A quick, teen-sized history snippet is that Madrid, Toledo, and Sevilla were supposedly the three main cities during the Golden Age. We can go see all of them if we have time!"

"When was the Golden Age?" Ryan asked, still wiping the sleep from his eyes as we piled into the taxi. "And what was so golden about it?"

"The Spanish Golden Age started around the year 1500 with the reign of King Ferdinand and Queen Isabel. It was near the end of the Reconquista, when there were battles within Spain to take back territory lost to conquerors in the centuries before, and to reestablish Catholicism as the main religion," Mr. García said. "What was golden about it was the art, music, literature, and even architecture that were created during that time, much of which we still enjoy today. Maybe you've heard of the famous artists Velázquez and El Greco? Or the novel *Don Quixote*?"

Ryan shook his head no, but Nic piped up excitedly, "Wow, I've seen some pictures of El Greco paintings in my art class—I had no idea they were painted that long ago, they look edgy!"

"Ah, a wonderful Spanish artist! If you've only seen copies of his paintings, you'll be even more amazed when you see the real thing at the Prado. Quick, everyone, look to the left!" Mr. García boomed happily.

We all turned to look to the left as our taxi sped past a huge and very beautiful red brick building.

"That is the Casa de la Panadería in the Plaza Mayor, which is one of Madrid's central and most important plazas, constructed in Spain's Golden Age. We must visit later—there are many shops and restaurants for us to enjoy," Mrs. García added.

"Wait—did you say Casa de la Panadería? 'The house of bread?'" I asked excitedly.

"Very good, Ruby! It was the city's main bakery, run by the baker's guild," Mr. García said. "Although I don't think there has been a working bakery there in centuries. Still, the Spanish do love their bread! Now, the entire plaza is like a marketplace from years ago, with vendors selling crafts, paintings, and souvenirs. Lots to choose from!"

Yup, Spain and I are going to get along just fine, I thought, looking around the beautiful city more. Surprisingly, much of what we drove past was very Westernized, with Starbucks and McDonald's signs on several corners, but it still didn't disappoint.

When we finally stepped out of the taxi in front of
a large, archaic, iron-gated door, it was so blazing hot
outside, I felt like a broiling chili pepper. The thick heat
practically pushed me back as I tried to look up at the
carvings on the Garcías' apartment building façade.

We stepped into the apartment building foyer, which,
despite smelling ancient, was spacious and cool enough
for all of us to spread out with our luggage and enjoy the
indoor respite. The creaky, ornate elevator was so tiny that
we had to split into several teams just to get up to the third
floor with all our luggage, even with Ryan and Nino racing
each other up the stairs instead.

From the elevator, we queued up in the narrow hallway
as Mr. García flipped through his giant keys, trying to open
the door. The keys were heavy and ornate, and apparently
hard to use.

When we finally filed in, I felt like I was in New York
City. The apartment was small but organized. The musty,
ancient smell that perfumed the entire building mixed with
the fresh dust layered on the plastic furniture covers. The
bathrooms were larger than in NYC, but had a weird stair
or step up to the shower stall. I guess I shouldn't say weird,
since my mom's NYC friend had a shower stall right in
the middle of the kitchen, with an actual door next to the
kitchen sink! The Madrid kitchen was tiny, with an unusual

dishwasher and a washer/dryer in one machine.

I couldn't wait to snoop around and see what types of tools and tricks the cupboards contained with which to whip up authentic Spanish food, but as soon as we all filed into our rooms and fell onto our bunk beds, I realized how wiped I was.

"Don't fall asleep, kids. We have to stay on schedule. We must maintain a schedule. We have a great deal to accomplish. We are about six hours ahead of the States, so we need to get a move on!" Mrs. García muttered, scuttling around.

I turned my head to Isabel, who was flopped onto her own mattress. "What does your mom mean? What do we have to accomplish?"

Isabel wearily shrugged her shoulders. "I don't know. Mom seems stressed and preoccupied with something. Who knows. I need to sleep."

I struggled to keep my eyes open as I watched my friend close hers and immediately fall asleep. I could still hear Mrs. García prowling along, taking the covers off furniture and getting the apartment in order for our stay.

"*Mi dulce*," I heard Mr. García murmur softly to his wife, "the children are exhausted from the flight and the excitement and this heat. Most of the shops will be closed for now, anyway, and even the tías will probably be napping. Let's all enjoy one of the traditions of this country—the siesta. Later, we can celebrate our arrival in true Spanish style—with tapas!"

I could hear Mrs. García protesting reluctantly, but Mr. García and my heavy eyelids must have won.

Chapter 4

Breathtaking Barrio

Jet-lag took most of us out with "siestas" that
actually lasted all the way through the night. When we woke
up the next morning, Nic informed us that he and Guille
had watched over us as Mr. and Mrs. García went out to pick
up a few tapas to celebrate our first night in Spain. The four
of them had enjoyed real Spanish tapas while the rest of us
were sleeping—now we had some catching up to do! All I
knew was that I was on the verge of hangry again, and tapas
translated to appetizers translated to food.

Once we were all up and ready, we headed out to the
bus stop a few blocks away. Several buses zipped by us, all
with different numbers and colors that were somewhat
dizzying. Before long, though, Mr. García hauled us on
to the right one, and we were on our way to the tías'
apartment.

32

"Don't forget, 'the tías' are actually my great-tías, my abuelo's sisters. One of my tías, Lorena, can understand and speak English pretty well. Another, Carla, can understand and speak broken English. Tía Paula can somewhat understand English, but cannot speak it at all. But that doesn't stop them from speaking all at once!" Isabel reminded me as we sped along.

The tías lived on a wide boulevard; their beautiful building must have been historical because it was in one of the oldest neighborhoods of Madrid. The street had lots of stops to the metro stations and those roundabouts like they have in Boston.

When we finally got to their apartment, we were met with another huge door with another giant key. Of course, there was another really old elevator in the lobby, even scarier than the Garcías', but we braved it.

The tías opened the nine-foot-tall door to greet us with smiles and kisses, beaming and doling out hugs (*abrazos*).

Isabel quickly whispered to me, "They haven't changed a bit!"

They were dressed just like you would expect: grandmotherly, with pearls around their necks, little earrings, and silk blouses. The three of them wore long skirts just past their knees, and little, black, old-fashioned shoes with thick heels that looked like they would be hard to walk in, but they managed to scurry around quickly. At first glance, they looked frail, but I saw right away they had lots of energy. They all wore red lipstick and big, warm smiles.

Tía Lorena, the oldest of all the tías and tíos, had her own apartment; she was visiting for our first greeting. Her hair was a wavy mahogany-brown, and she wore gold bangle bracelets that matched her tawny gold silk blouse. Isabel had told me Tía Carla was a former paralegal; her eyes were lively and quick as they took in the young boys pushing each other toward the candy dish. Her shiny silver mane draped down over the top of a beautiful black and white silk scarf that was tied perfectly around her neck. Tía Paula had short coffee-brown hair and wore a two-strand pearl necklace with matching pearl earrings. Tía Lorena and Carla seemed tiny at five-two—until you saw Tía Paula, who, at four-ten, was as small as Ryan!

When the tías had finished their hugs and everything had calmed down, they ushered everyone into the front parlor to sit on ornate antique furniture. While the grown-ups talked, I got a better look at the apartment. The entryway had dark stained wood floors that creaked when we walked and ceilings twenty feet high. It reminded me of Isabel's house, but much older. The walls were vibrantly colored, and they had very large paintings of people hanging on them. There were, of course, lots of

34

photographs, but most were black and white with antique frames.

Ryan and Nino ran to the tall windows and peered out over the balcony down to the streets. Guille explained that these traditional-style balconies are called *miradores*; they face the main street on which apartments are located and are great for people watching. Of course, Mrs. García had to pull them back into the apartment once they began to yell, "Hello down there" to the innocent pedestrians below. The boys quickly found their attention diverted to more candies on the coffee table.

I noticed one of the tías pointing to me and heard, "Chinita."

Mrs. García nodded in agreement and clarified. "Ruby, they are complimenting your almond-shaped eyes and almond complexion."

I hadn't thought of my complexion as almond-colored. Isabel and her brothers all had that perfectly smooth sesame complexion.

I walked over with Isabel to the grown-up table while everyone spoke Spanish. Mrs. García and Tía Lorena were huddled in a secluded corner, speaking softly just to each other, but Tía Carla and Tía Paula were giving a history lesson to Guille, Isabel, and Nino. Mr. García explained that the tías were naming some of the Spanish regions to the

kids, ensuring that they appreciated Spain's geography and culture, especially since Spain is quite different from region to region.

"Even Spain's cuisine is regional . . . the food of the Basque Country in the north is different from that of Andalusia, the southernmost region of Spain. In Galicia, the northwest region of the country that includes several provinces with coastline, you can find *empanada gallega*, a delicious pastry you can fill with whatever you want, like meat or vegetables, and they have a spicy dish served with potatoes and octopus on top that is *riquísimo*, delicious." Mr. García translated for us as Tía Paula explained. "In the Castilla-La Mancha region of central Spain, the *cochinillo*, or roast pig, can be found all over, and is mouthwatering when roasted just right."

I leaned over to Ryan and whispered, "That is just like *doong* or *zongzi*—each province in China makes it differently. Like little stories wrapped in lotus leaves."

Ryan looked up. "Dung? We don't eat dung—isn't that poop?"

I rolled my eyes and shook my head. "Not dung, *doong*—the lotus leaves filled with sticky rice. It's your favorite."

Tía Carla, who spoke some English, nodded and added, "The beauty of Spain is from sea to sea, el Atlántico, el mar Cantábrico, y el mar Mediterráneo."

Tía Lorena looked up from her conversation with Mrs. García to add, "There is cultural beauty within, too—the masters Velazquez, Goya, El Greco, y Murillo."

Nic whispered to Mr. García, "I am catching most of what they say, but they speak so quickly . . . I heard something about Goya again; where does that fit in?"

Mr. García smiled. "Yes, we began discussing the Spanish masters the moment we stepped foot off the plane! That is one of my favorite topics—art! The Spanish people are very proud of their country, especially their art and literature. When we visit the Prado, we'll stop in to appreciate Goya's masterpieces. You like art?"

I missed Nic's response as I began eavesdropping on Mrs. García's conversation with Tía Lorena.

"*Hice una lista de algunos alimentos que a mi amigo le gustaría probar y busqué en mi teléfono algunos restaurantes cercanos. ¿Qué te parece, Tía?*"

I couldn't understand what they were talking about, but I understood enough to know they were talking about restaurants! My stomach was grumbling loudly, and I couldn't concentrate on anything but tapas now, so I was glad to hear we were going out to eat. It was already nearly two in the afternoon, and we hadn't gotten lunch yet!

The tías huddled together to discuss; once they

decided which restaurant could accommodate all of us, we regrouped out on the boulevard sidewalk, surrounded by blaring horns. We walked about two blocks from the apartment into a little restaurant.

The tías knew the maître d', and he sat us right away. The waiters brought out several little dishes of sausages, which Nino and Ryan devoured. Tía Lorena motioned to stop the boys from eating so many sausages—she was worried they would get upset stomachs when there were many tapas to eat.

Ryan groaned loudly about how hungry he was, and Mr. García laughed.

"I'm sorry, Ryan, I should have explained—Spaniards eat late lunches, but it's the most important meal of the day. Then you can have a siesta, wake up to *merendar* (snack), and have dinner later, around nine or ten in the evening. You will be stuffed by the time the day is finished."

Within a few minutes, the table started filling up with plates of stewed mixed vegetables (*pisto*), a breaded and fried appetizer filled with ham and olives (*croquetas de jamón y aceituna* filled with béchamel), an egg and potato pie (*tortilla de patatas*), a dumpling, but bigger and shaped differently (*empanadillas*), shrimp (*gambas*), mussels (*mejillones*), anchovies, (*boquerones*), Spanish sausage (chorizo), white asparagus, and fresh bread.

39

Suddenly, the table erupted in argument!

I looked around, confused, but Isabel explained that was the normal course of business—"Grown-ups, especially the tías, always excitedly discuss the conventionalism of the *pisto* and the *croquetas* as they are served."

I raised an eyebrow at Isabel. "The conventionalism?"

Isabel laughed. "Oh, you know—first, of course, the presentation; second, whether it is standard or traditional, sort of like those cooking shows. But here, since all the tías and tíos cook the dish, the croquetas have to be just the right size, and then the tortilla has to be just the perfect texture . . ." Isabel paused, listening intently for a second. "Wait, wait one minute! They are all up in arms about the pisto!"

"Why? It looks amazing! I have had pisto at your house, and it usually looks a lot like that—except I don't ever remember your mom serving it with sausage," I said.

"That's just it—pisto is a vegetable dish, although it can be served with a fried egg on top. Since the restaurant has sliced chorizo in their pisto, the tías are arguing it is not pisto at all. They want to send it back to the kitchen for a traditional pisto. Tía Paula is saying that even advertising the tapas as pisto then adding chorizo is a travesty." Isabel laughed, amused by the scandal. "This is a first, Ruby; log it. The culprit tapas are usually the croquetas or the tortilla."

By the time we finished eating nearly three hours later, the pisto incident was behind us and everyone was satisfied. We finally exited the restaurant and exchanged kisses, or *besos*, and found a taxi back to the Garcías' apartment.

When we got back to our rooms, Ryan announced, "I can't believe we heard all about that history stuff—art, food, regions, and everything—and no one talked about bullfighting!" He grabbed a red shirt from his suitcase and started waving it around. "When do we get to run from the bulls? Olé!"

I rolled my eyes as Nino ran at the red shirt, pretending to be an angry bull, and the boys crashed around, laughing and goofing off. Brothers!

Chapter 5

Perplexing Prado

The next day, I woke up early, ready to get my girl thing going and do some shopping. I couldn't wait to hit the Spanish markets and find extra special gifts for my Gong Gong and PoPo—I just hoped I had enough money saved from my allowance to buy a souvenir or two for myself!

Most of my travel crew seemed preoccupied, though. That wasn't new for Mrs. García—she'd been in her own world since we'd gotten off the plane. She'd definitely been unusually short with everyone (no pun intended), and Isabel seemed really worried about her. But now, Mr. García was upset because he hadn't able to get special exhibit tickets at the Museo del Prado. Both Nino and Ryan were brooding, too, because they had heard bullfighting was no longer an option because of concerns for the welfare of the bulls. Only Nic, Guille, and I seemed ready to conquer

Madrid and anything that came our way.

Eventually, we managed to convince everyone to head out and explore, and we started with a walk along the Calle de Gran Vía. There were so many souvenir shops and clothing stores I was almost overwhelmed. Luckily, I had my best friend in tow!

We stumbled on the perfect shop that had every knickknack and tchotchke imaginable. My PoPo loves tchotchkes! My mom does not—she loathes trinkets of any kind. Luckily, since she would be in Spain herself soon, I didn't have to buy her a gift! I found a *Don Quixote* hotplate and the quintessential Spanish wooden spoon for Gong Gong and a beautiful, hand-painted ceramic ladle for PoPo to hold her tea ball.

Suddenly, I turned the corner in the shop and found a whole wall dedicated to hand-painted ceramic pottery; Mr. García was already there eyeing several pieces.

"What are these dishes? They are so pretty! I want all of them, but I don't think they will fit in my luggage! Plus, my mom will flip a lid if I get a bunch of pottery trinkets," I said.

Mr. García laughed. "Well, you can't fit all of this in your luggage . . . but one critical piece of pottery you *must* buy is the tortilla dish. You see, *para volver la tortilla*. This dish was crafted specifically for the tortilla! It has a foot so that you can skillfully toss your tortilla from the pan directly onto this plate."

43

Comically, Mr. García was demonstrating how to turn the tortilla, his arms flailing everywhere. I saw Isabel give me a baffled expression from across the shop, and then she motioned for me to join her.

"Thanks, Mr. García!" I grabbed the plate and placed it in my basket as I sprinted toward Isabel.

Isabel covered her face with her hands and groaned. "Oh my gosh, he is so embarrassing!"

We both started giggling as we hurried down the stairs and out of sight. "Just wait until my dad gets here! Between his jokes and your dad's antics, it's complete embarrassment across two continents!"

In the basement of the souvenir shop, Isabel found the end of the rainbow—sports jerseys for Real Madrid and Rafael Nadal! She was in athletic heaven. I bought a pencil sharpener and holder, plus a cute notebook for myself that said "Vive Positivo" across the front. I was quite pleased with my plunder!

Finally, Mr. García said, "All right, everyone. Let's head on out to the Prado. They have many masterpieces that boys and girls should appreciate."

Skeptically, we all piled out the door and to the metro stop. Fortunately, the lines were short, and we moved through the lobby of the museum quickly. Mr. García scanned the map and began circling all the different collections he wanted to see.

"Don't worry. I can tell by your faces that you are losing interest already. This isn't the Louvre. We can see most of the paintings within a short period," Mrs. García whispered.

Ryan turned to Nino. "What is the Loov?"

Nino replied, "I thought he said the loo. Isn't that 'bathroom' in French?"

They both started laughing and chanting, "Loo rhymes with poo!" as they walked over to the lobby gift shop.

Even though many of the paintings and sculptures were really impressive, it didn't take long for me to wish that I'd joined Ryan and Nino in the gift shop. I was surprised by how excited Mr. García could get about each piece, and he did the best job possible explaining interesting history and facts to put them in context. What I was most shocked by, however, was that Nic hung on every word and seemed really interested in every painting.

Later, standing in front of what looked like dried pastry icing on a large black painting of an old ghost-like figure, Mr. García commented, "See, kids! Just like in your Percy Jackson books by Rick Riordan? Remember when they bring Cronos back to life, and then he eats everyone? Not only are you standing in a museum that was first opened in 1819, but

45

this piece by the important Spanish artist Goya dates back to around 1820. How does that make you feel, standing here with art that has transcended time? It draws you in and can either envelop or repel you with its darkness."

Both Guille and Isabel shrugged their shoulders. "Cool. I guess."

Ryan replied, "Who is Rio-ordinian?"

Nic shot Ryan a look. "You read Percy Jackson with Mom . . . remember?"

Guille patted his dad on the shoulder. "I remember those books, Dad. I loved mythology when I was little."

I nudged Isabel, whispering, "Ask if there is a café on this floor. I am starving."

"I'm with you," Mrs. García murmured quietly. "Let's go find a bite to eat."

With the exception of Mr. García and Nic, everyone trailed behind us as we walked away in search of food.

I turned to Isabel. "Your poor dad. Everyone but Nic left him. They're just standing there reading his Prado guide book."

Guille laughed. "Don't worry about them. Dad is in his element. He loves his books."

Guille was right. The rest of us circled back around to find Mr. García and Nic once we had finished our snacks, but they had joined up with a tour group and were enthralled with all the additional historical and artistic facts at the museum. Shaking our heads, we told them to catch up when they were ready and stepped outside to explore some of the major plazas on scooters.

★ ★ ★

Of course, before we'd even left the States, Mom had insisted we set up a time to talk and share our adventures with her and Dad each day. Ryan, Nic, and I each provided our own updates during the nightly calls at 9:00 p.m. Nic's updates seemed to be more art and architecture focused, and Ryan was a wildcard—he seemed to develop a new interest each day, just to drop it for something fresh and exciting the next. Mine were usually about the food, which was easy—I not only had the day's lunch to fill them in on, but I was also usually starving for dinner, since we usually went out to eat right after the call! I could get used to a lot of things, but I didn't think I could ever get used to the Spanish eating schedule.

This evening, though, when we got on the phone, Mom had news of her own to share. On her insistence, the three of us crowded around the speakerphone together.

"Guess what?" Mom said excitedly. "Gong Gong has been invited to go to Boston. The City of Boston's

archaeologist, Tom Smith, is planning a historic archaeological dig in Boston's Chinatown right at the exact address of your great grandmother's former restaurant, Ruby Foo's Den, at 6 Hudson Street!"

She mentioned that the dig was tentatively scheduled for August, right before school started, so hopefully, we could all drive up to Boston together for the celebration. I couldn't believe it—more family history to be unveiled! Maybe I'd have an extra credit project for Mrs. Zecker with NJHS after all!

Ryan excitedly said, "Mom, isn't Massachusetts famous for their lobster? I ate a sardine. It was so salty and fishy I felt sick."

I sighed. "It was an anchovy, not a sardine."

Mom replied, "Oh no. I've read about those, little *boquerones*. Well, don't worry, Ryan, Boston has lobster. Maine is known for Maine lobsters. I am certain Boston has plenty of lobster, too!"

Ryan sighed. "What a relief; I love lobster rolls."

I rolled my eyes and kicked my brothers off the line so I could fill Mom in on the other major food events of the day. After souvenir shopping and the Prado, they'd let us choose our lunch spot. After much deliberation, we settled on the Mercado de San Miguel for tapas.

Walking into the square-shaped indoor market, we were

49

greeted by delicious aromas from more than fifty vendors; we quickly scattered to gather our individual favorites and met at an outside table overlooking the main street.

Using my phone photos, a quick review of our selections revealed sandwiches (*bocadillos*) of every type— prawns (*de camarones*), squid (*de calamares*), cod (*de bacalao*), and shrimp (*de gambas*). We were clearly all hungry for seafood! Ryan and Nino had also wisely chosen *bocadillos de calamares*, and there were various olive-skewered kebabs and croquetas filled with a sauce called béchamel and either cod, ham, shrimp, or olives. We stuffed ourselves, and of course, we did a taste test. Surprisingly, the cod croquetas won!

Mom was excited to hear about our food adventures, and she made me promise to take her back to get more of the cod croquetas when she and Dad reached Madrid. Since my parents only had a few days to see Spain, they had decided to fly into Seville because they wanted to see the cathedral, the largest Gothic building in the world. We would meet them there, and afterward, we'd all take the train back to Madrid together. My mom ended the conversation the same way she did every night—"Please stay on your best behavior. We miss you and will see you all very soon in Seville!"

As soon as I hung up the phone, I raced in to see what the plan was for dinner. When I saw that only Isabel and her mom were left in the apartment, I instantly got fuming mad. I couldn't believe that Nic and Ryan had left for dinner without me!

Isabel laughed, then explained, "No, Mom told them to go ahead. Apparently, our super-top-secret girls' trip begins tonight!"

Isabel had been making fun, but Mrs. García didn't seem to notice. It didn't seem possible, but she was even more distracted and worried-looking than she'd been for the entire trip.

"Mmm, well, grab your things, girls," Mrs. García said. "We're going to have a sleepover at Tía Lorena's apartment near Barrio de las Letras so we can set out first thing tomorrow morning."

"Where are we going?" Isabel asked.

"Hmm?" Mrs. García was distracted by her phone.

Isabel rolled her eyes. "For like the fifth time, where are we going on this trip? Why aren't the guys coming?"

"Segovia," Mrs. García snapped. "Tía Lorena and I are meeting a . . . a friend for lunch at a hotel in Segovia, just an hour or so from Madrid. The boys aren't coming because we need some quiet. I thought you and Ruby would enjoy coming along and having a picnic and enjoying the landscape there, but if you don't think you can behave yourselves . . ."

Isabel and I exchanged glances. Mrs. García really wasn't acting like her usual self.

"No, Mom, that sounds good," Isabel said quietly.

Throughout the ride, Isabel chatted excitedly about Tía Lorena's apartment and Barrio de las Letras, obviously trying to draw her mom into the conversation: "Dad told me this is where all the great writers and artists lived during the Spanish Golden Age, including Cervantes!"

Mrs. García was silent, staring out the windows as we turned off the wide boulevards and into the narrow streets of the neighborhood. Isabel and I looked at each other and shrugged.

"Oh, I overheard your brothers talking about Boston after they got off the phone—are you guys taking another trip?" Isabel asked.

I swallowed hard. I wanted to tell my best friend about the newest development in my hunt for family history, but I also felt bad. Here Isabel was in her own family's country, and her mom wouldn't even tell her what was happening tomorrow! I knew she still didn't have any more information for her extra credit assignment, and I didn't want to make her feel bad.

Luckily, just then, we arrived at Tía Lorena's apartment. Mrs. García and Tía Lorena disappeared together to talk the moment we walked in, but Isabel walked me around the apartment and showed me all the cool things it was filled with, collected from throughout the country. My favorite was the real stuffed fox head, *cabeza de zorro*, that hung from the wall, showing its teeth with a menacing snarl. Isabel shuttered and proceeded to tell me how Guille had always intentionally tormented her with Zorro whenever the lights were out.

"I think there's more in the storage room, but I've never been allowed in there," Isabel said, touching a doorknob tentatively.

Looking back down the hall to the door her mom and tía had partially shut behind them, Isabel seemed to be struggling with an idea. She motioned for me to stay put, and she tip-toed to her tía's door to eavesdrop. I was impressed by her agile, light-footed movements and the silent perch she assumed to hold her ear to the door and peek in—but they must have heard something, because all of a sudden, the door shut completely.

In a split second, Isabel pounced back next to me. She straightened herself up to her full height and whispered bravely, "They're busy! Let's go look!"

I almost warned her about the last time I'd gone poking around where people store old things—Gong Gong's attic—and accidentally dug up a whole mystery. But I was

53

curious, too, and since that story had ended happily, I just shrugged and tiptoed behind her. We crawled through a small cubby door into the stuffed storage room. Luggage and books and trinkets and antiques were piled to the ceiling.

"Your great-aunt must have traveled a lot," I said, admiring all her things.

"I know Tía Lorena has been all around Spain, but I'm not sure she's ever even left the country. It's weird—there's a lot about her that no one talks about, and we have always been shushed when certain subjects came up. Like, I'm pretty sure she used to be married, but I know nothing of that tío. I once asked her where he was, and Mom rushed me away so fast, I thought she'd run me straight back across the ocean!" Isabel replied.

I nodded. "I get that—after all, we're *just* starting to learn about Gong Gong's childhood."

"Yeah," Isabel muttered, "adults keep a lot of secrets. But Tía Lorena has always been one of my favorite tías—I'm really hoping I can catch her alone at some point and ask her about our family history so I have something to report back to Mrs. Zecker. Tía Lorena has never let me down—she always has something special for me. Like when I was little, she had unicorn coloring books with rainbow-colored markers and glitter glue waiting for me whenever we visited. I mean, my other tías are cool, too; they usually give me Real Madrid clothes and keychains—which I obviously love."

"You and your soccer." I interrupted, executing one of my better eye-rolls. "I'll never get it. But it's no wonder you're so good—those catlike reflexes are impressive! I can't believe they almost caught you."

Isabel grinned momentarily at the compliment, but then her face got really serious. "They must be on high alert—I wish I could have heard more. My tía was saying something about being worried about misunderstandings. You should have seen how tightly she was holding my mom's hand!"

"Do you think it has anything to do with why your mom is so grouchy?" I asked.

"It definitely seems like Mom is helping Tía Lorena with something, but I don't know any more than you do," Isabel said, shaking her head with frustration as she grabbed an old, leather satchel from a corner. "I forgot my backpack at our apartment—I think I'll borrow this one for our trip since I don't want to lug my notebook and stuff around in my arms."

Just then, we heard sounds from across the hall and realized we needed to get out of the storage room fast. We dashed back into the hallway, under the watchful eye of Zorro, just in the nick of time.

Chapter 6

Secretive Segovia

Mrs. García seemed surprised enough when she caught us in the hallway. "I thought I sent you two to bed?"

Isabel and I looked at each other and shook our heads.

"Well, I meant to," she barked before firmly demanding we immediately settle into our sleeping bags. "Early start tomorrow! No delays!"

Once the lights were out, Isabel whispered, "See? My mom is never that short, yelling at us like that."

"Maybe we'll find out more tomorrow in Segovia," I whispered back, trying to assure my friend. Honestly, I was just glad she hadn't caught us snooping!

I closed my eyes and tried not to think of Guille's insistence that Zorro awoke at night and prowled the halls, looking for anyone deeply asleep to eat. I was positive I wouldn't sleep at all.

I was wrong, though. I woke up to another bright Madrid sunrise and the smell of something delicious cooking. Isabel and I scrambled toward the kitchen, where Tía Lorena immediately served us *chocolate caliente* con pan. My eyes widened—I rarely ate sweets for breakfast at home—but Isabel and Tía Lorena both assured me that Spanish hot chocolate and bread was a perfectly respectable breakfast. I watched as Isabel proceeded to spread Nutella on her bread in addition to dipping it in her hot cocoa. My best friend is a genius. Of course, I tried it. What's not to like? It's chocolate *con* chocolate.

"Mmm. Will you teach us how to make this bread while we're here?" I asked. "Is this a family recipe? Did you know how to cook like this when you were our age?"

For once, Isabel didn't tell me to stop peppering my questions. But Tía Lorena got a funny look on her face, and Mrs. García began speaking to Tía Lorena again in rapid-fire Spanish, as if we didn't exist. Isabel and I looked at each other and shrugged—we'd have to get more answers later.

The second we were finished with breakfast, Tía Lorena and Mrs. García appeared in the doorway with blankets, sunglasses, and pillows for the trip. Aurelia, Tía Lorena's assistant, would be our driver. We packed into the car and started counting all the strange, cowboy-shaped billboards

along the road, but by the time we'd got to our third cowboy, I'd fallen back asleep.

I woke up the moment we arrived at our destination—which was apparently Segovia. I could see the amazing Roman aqueduct as we made our way to the Marador, a hotel for the secret meeting. Lucky for us, the hotel rested on a hillside overlooking the city.

"There are many myths and legends that surround Segovia's Roman aqueduct. It was built two-thousand years ago, but it was still a working water system when my great-grandparents were children! It brought water from the Sierra de Guadarrama into the city. Madrid still has the best-tasting water in all of Spain because it comes from those mountains," Aurelia said.

"Issy, take Ruby and the picnic basket to the vista since it's such a beautiful day. Your Tía Lorena and I are going to have a *café* inside and meet a friend for lunch in the hotel restaurant. You two don't need to sit around with us. When we're done, I will text you," Mrs. García said firmly as we all arrived at the hotel and scrambled out of the car.

As the adults marched into the hotel, Isabel and I debated whether we should sneak in and see who their mysterious meeting was with. Clearly, the adults were on a mission of their own. We waited a few minutes, but were ushered out by the hotel maître d'. I was excited to get a better look at the aqueducts, so I convinced Isabel we could come back and catch them in the act before lunch was even done. We finally walked out to the patio and climbed over the brick fence. We laid out the blanket and gaped at the vista of the beautiful town over the rolling hills.

Tía Lorena's picnic basket turned out to be an absolute treasure trove of food. Isabel unwrapped baguettes that had been rubbed with fresh tomatoes and sprinkled with olive oil, salt, and pepper before they'd been piled with *jamón serrano*. Paired with bags of chips and containers of olives and manchego, it was heavenly.

After the big lunch, we lounged out to the take in the full beauty of Segovia. Isabel, sunglasses on, leaned her head against the old, leather satchel she'd borrowed from Tía Lorena's storage room. I could hear her breathing starting to get heavier, and I was drowsy, too—the combination of the hot sun and the massive midday meal really was a perfect recipe for a nap.

"Hey, Isabel, don't go to sleep quite yet. I threw my notebook in the satchel this morning—let me grab it; I want to sketch the aqueducts," I said.

Isabel groaned and sat up, opening up the bag and rooting around for my notebook and pencil. "I barely slept last night. Kept looking for Zorro. I think we're going to be playing fútbol with my cousins tomorrow—I need all the sleep I can get."

She settled back onto the satchel-pillow, and I opened my journal and flipped through to a clean page. As soon as I started the sketch, I could already tell it was going to be one of my best yet. This place was some kind of magic.

Snap.

And there went my pencil tip.

I looked over at Isabel, sound asleep, and wondered what to do.

Two lizards scurried past me as I quietly took apart the picnic basket, hoping to find something—a sharpener, another pencil, even a pen! Nothing.

I took a deep breath and shook my best friend awake. Even though she had sunglasses on, I could tell she wasn't pleased. But hey, we'd have all the time in the world to sleep when we returned from Spain!

"Can you look for another pencil or a knife or something in the bag?"

Grumbling, Isabel tore through the leather satchel like a very sleepy bear on a rampage. "There's nothing in here, I checked before we left the apartm—"

The *rip* of the lining coming away from the inside of the bag was so loud, I could swear it echoed across the gorgeous landscape. Isabel and I looked at each other, frozen in panic.

"Tía Lorena's going to be so disappointed with me. My mom is going to punish me," Isabel groaned, turning the bag inside out so we could inspect the damage. The inner liner had torn neatly and completely in half.

"We can probably fix that if we can find a needle—I was watching my mom when she sewed those pockets; that seems easy to clean up!" I said.

"Look, Ruby—it's been cut and sewn up before." Isabel poked at the liner, then stuck her hand inside the hole. "There's something in here!"

I watched as she pulled out a small folded square of paper.

"I can speak Spanish, but I'm not great at reading it. Okay . . . 'Rob' . . . something . . . 'practice and you' . . . something? Signed with a scribble, looks like 'Huva' . . ."

I started laughing again. "What's 'Huva'? Sounds quirky, but it's even weirder that someone went through the trouble of stitching it away!"

"Maybe there's more in here—like the key to my family history I've been looking for!" Isabel patted and pawed inside the liner, looking for anything else. Suddenly, she made a strange face and pulled out the entire bottom of the bag, ripping the liner to shreds.

"What are you doing?! There's no way we can stitch

leather back together!" I cried.

Isabel shook her head, examining the weirdly bunched-up hunk of dry, cracked leather in her hands. "No, Ruby, this was just . . . in there. It wasn't attached."

"What is it?" I asked, running a finger down the patchwork of leather shapes stitched together. "A map, maybe? A pelt?"

Isabel turned it over and laughed at me. "Ruby, this is a very old fútbol."

"Oh, well, no wonder that old satchel was so heavy," I said, yawning and lying back on the blanket. "That's not really a treasure—you've got tons of new soccer balls at home. Pack it back in the bag from lunch; we can throw it out when we get back to the hotel."

Isabel didn't say anything. When I opened my eyes, she was sitting quietly, staring at the note and hugging the fútbol tightly. I raised up my sunglasses and gave her a curious look.

"Your preeeciousss?"

Isabel laughed loudly, scaring away a few more of the lizards who had approached our picnic site. "You know Tolkien is one of my favorites."

I smiled at her. "Of course I do. But that slab of decaying leather isn't exactly the One Ring."

Isabel shook her head. "I don't know, Ruby. It feels special. Why else would Tía Lorena have it hidden in her storage room, sewn up into this old bag? Who is Rob?"

"Maybe Tía Lorena was a spy. Or a time traveler. Or . . ."

Isabel shrugged. "It makes as much sense as anything else. My family is so proud of their culture and their country, but they never talk about their history. You've seen how strange my mom has been acting on this trip, Ruby. Every time I try to ask her what's wrong, she dodges it and then tries to distract me."

I teased her. "So, now your mom is a time-traveling spy, too? Her top-secret technique is 'dodge and distract?' Oh!" I exclaimed, sitting straight up. "What about their mysterious friend? Maybe your mom has been stressed about meeting with a spy for the other side . . ."

Isabel rolled her eyes. "Very funny. But we've been out here forever—we should run back and see who they are meeting with."

We scrambled to pack up the picnic blanket and sprinted back to the hotel, but when we got there, the entire restaurant was empty. For a minute, we panicked and wondered if we'd accidentally been left behind. Finally, though, we spied Aurelia, Tía Lorena, and Mrs. García on the balcony, flipping through a book. When we ran up to them, Mrs. García quickly closed the book and zipped it into her bag. Still kind of suspicious, but they all had smiles on their faces and seemed relaxed. Mrs. García was definitely in a much better mood than she'd been . . . well, for our entire trip!

I think Isabel was trying to figure out how to bring up our discovery when the adults dropped the real bombshell: apparently, Isabel had missed her mom's text to come in and have *cochinillo asado*, Segovia's traditional dish of a whole roasted suckling pig. Both Isabel and I stewed the whole car ride home that we had missed out on what is supposed to be the regional specialty, a dish fit for royalty.

Chapter 7

Pueblo Paella Party

The next major trip on our itinerary was a visit to another side of Isabel's family who lived on the outskirts of Madrid in a small pueblo called Colmenarejo. We climbed onto the bus to take a forty-minute ride out to the calming suburbs, and I sat in the first seat I could find near the window. I sat next to Nic, whose Spanish music boomed from his earbuds as he proceeded to fall asleep annoyingly on my shoulder. Isabel sat with her mom, still trying to find a good opportunity to bring up our mysterious Segovia discovery. Mrs. García had been in a much better mood since we'd returned from our girls' trip, but she'd firmly shut down any questions we'd asked about her mysterious meeting, even telling us not to mention it to Mr. García and the boys. Despite some work, time-traveling spy was still our best guess!

With just a few miles left to go, the hills revealed homes peppered across them, and the bus had to stop for a herd of goats. We got off the bus and were met by more tías and cousins at the curb. They ushered us into the house where we were quickly bombarded by Isabel's family and caught up in what she later called *cárcel de besos*—a prison of kisses. Everyone exchanged double kisses on the cheeks.

Great-Tío Francisco was the youngest of her abuelo's six siblings. From the photos I'd seen at Isabel's house, they looked identical, with the same warm smiles and kind eyes. Great-Tío Francisco and Great-Tía Jimena held hands while they proudly introduced their family to us. They had five children: Tía Martena, who was married to Tío Manuel and had Carolina and twins Daniel and Mateo; Tío Diego, who was married to Tía Valentina and had two kids, Lucia and Diego; Tía Francisca, who was married to Tío Jose and had a daughter, Luna; Tío Antonio, who was married to Tía Mariana and had two girls, Mariana and Lena; and their youngest daughter, Tía Jimena. All the cousins were in college, except Diego, who had only one year left of high school.

Before roll call was even fully completed, Great-Tía Jimena hurried back to the kitchen, throwing on her apron over her wavy, silver-gray short hair. She wore dark brown pants and a pragmatic cotton shirt with rolled-up sleeves to prep for lunch. Soon, all her daughters were in the kitchen alongside her. Tía Martena stood cutting vegetables, Tía Francisca was opening a can of olives, and Tía Jimena had her hands full of plates. All of them had the same dark saffron-colored hair. Tía Jimena immediately directed Mrs. García to the cutting board and began instructing her on how to wash and cut octopus, or *pulpo*.

Isabel and I stood at attention, ready to jump into the mix and learn everything they could teach us about this kitchen, but Tía Martena motioned for us to go. When we hesitated, she took our hands and walked us outside! Before I knew it, one of the cousins had pulled us into a game of soccer.

All the cousins were Guille's age and older, but that didn't mean they were going to treat us like babies or even guests—the teasing started immediately.

Diego yelled out as he stole the ball from Ryan, "Modric from Real Madrid steals the ball and passes to Cousin Carolina from Barça!"

Daniel and Mateo, the twin brothers with wavy, espresso-colored hair, shouted, "From behind, Daniel from Bilbao steals from Carolina, shoots, and scores!"

Mariana yelled, "Go Bilbao!"

Everyone yelled, *"Gol, gol, gol."*

Picking up a garden pail, Mariana tapped it from the bottom.

Diego slid and passed to Guille, shouting, *"¡Modric buscando Bale!"*

Everyone started laughing, and several shouted, *"¡Tenemos nuestro propio Bombo!"*

I had no idea what was happening, so I turned to Lucia, who seemed the calmest of the cousins. I tried to decide which question to ask first before I landed on, "What is a '*bombo*?'"

She laughed. "Spain's most famous fútbol fan, Manolo. He travels to all the games beating on a drum."

Mateo laughed, "And Modric's a great player, but nothing like Juan Arza from Sevilla FC, the first real fútbol club in Spain!"

Diego was irritated. "Modric is more than just an attacking midfielder—he's smart with the ball! And Sevilla FC was not the first fútbol club—that was Huelva. Get your facts straight!"

The twins jokingly patted Diego on the head. *"Tranquilo, chico."*

"Are they angry with each other?" I asked Lucia.

"Oh no, Ruby. It is just fun and games, as you would say in the US. Here, fútbol rivalry is part of Spain and being Spanish! The rivalry between the fútbol clubs and the players is always serious fun. Everyone knows fútbol, especially the grandmothers!"

I looked at Isabel, who was smiling widely, and felt like I'd just started to understand why soccer—I mean, fútbol— was so important to her. It wasn't just the game itself, which, as I got into it, was much more fun than I'd thought. It was part of her family, part of her heritage. I even smiled at Ryan and Nic, who were holding their own and juggling the soccer ball between their feet with the rest of the kids. Being around so many siblings and cousins who were so close and enjoyed playing together so much reminded me that I was actually pretty lucky to have my own brothers here with me.

By the time the game ended, the outdoor table was set for twenty-seven people. Tío Diego and his son Diego stood manning their own paella pans on special stands with flames blowing from underneath.

I heard one of Isabel's cousins say, "*Nos vamos de paella*," but I wasn't sure I heard her correctly, so I asked Isabel, "Did she just say 'We're going for a paella'?"

"Yes—in Spain, 'We're going for a paella' doesn't just mean we are going to eat the dish. One of the most traditional ways to cook a paella is outside, over a campfire, with everyone around, so it's kind of like saying 'We're

71

going to a barbecue' back home," Isabel explained.

She was right—everyone stood around, laughing and chatting and watching as two different types of paellas were cooked: one all seafood, one chicken. Lucia stood by, translating all the ingredients for us and explaining the process. Nic, whose interest in food was almost exclusively the eating, not the cooking, stood nearby and listened, obviously impressed by the ease with which Diego moved around the paella. Next to Tío Diego stood both Guille and Mr. García, and they all spoke seriously about managing broth measurements and how the wind might affect the flames.

"The ratio for the broth to rice is more important than the other ingredients," noted Mr. García. "In the end, it's all about the rice."

"The timing of the rice requires patience and skill," remarked Tío Diego.

Suddenly, I noticed all the older cousins clustered at one side of the table, which had now been layered with appetizers.

Isabel ran up and pulled me over. "Hurry and sit down, you have to taste Tía Valentina's empanada and you have to try Tía Francisca's *croquetas con aceituna* before they disappear!"

"What should I eat first?" I panicked, quickly biting

into the piping hot croqueta in one hand and grabbing an empanada with the other.

Nino walked over, guiding Ryan, and they both grabbed some bread and sat down with their *sopa*.

"That," explained Isabel, "is Nino's favorite. It's called *salmorejo*. It looks like gazpacho, but it's not. Tía Jimena makes that, too."

"What's the difference? They both look like a tomato soup base," I said.

Lucia chimed in. "Very good, Ruby. They both have the tomato base, but locals tend to lean more toward the *salmorejo*, which has tomatoes, garlic, and bread. Gazpacho has tomatoes and other vegetables, but no bread. Both are delicious."

On the other end of the table, all the grown-ups sat chatting and eating stuffed olives and Spanish almonds.

Before long, the paellas were placed on the table. We all made a big fuss over them—they looked perfect. Isabel and I stopped chatting immediately and started taking notes and photos to post. The shimmering shellfish immediately added a "power punch presentation." I must have taken at least twenty pictures of the lobster, but looking at the chicken paella next to the seafood paella, I knew this was going to be a difficult choice.

73

Tío Diego took the wooden spoon and scraped the bottom of the pan for each serving. Everyone loves the golden crust of rice from the bottom of the paella pan. It reminded me of the burned rice at the bottom of the saucepan at my PoPo's house. She never uses a rice cooker because she likes the burned rice bottom. She even adds water to the bottom of the saucepan and boils it, then drinks it like tea. She calls it "fondil." I missed my PoPo, especially when visiting all of Isabel's tías and great-tías.

The table was quiet, everyone dug in, and then each person announced either "I like the chicken," or, "I like the seafood."

Finally, paella chef Tío Diego chimed in. "The seafood was good, but I think the rice was not perfect. It was slightly undercooked."

Before he could finish, Ryan shouted, "Therefore, it's *sliced*!" and he and Nino ran away laughing.

On our way back to the apartment, Mr. García polled us: "So, what do you think about Tío Diego's paella?"

"The mussels, clams, and lobster with beans add to the stylish presentation. And of course, it was delicious. But all in all, we agree that Tío Diego's chicken paella was almost as flavorsome as the seafood one," Isabel and I observed, consulting back and forth with each other and our notes.

Mr. García scratched his chin. "You girls are quite the food critics. Impressive evaluation. I agree. Although I love shrimp, and the pimientos add a great deal of flavor. Don't forget, the beans add serious texture."

"For texture, though, it's all about the crust of rice at the bottom of the pan, the *socarrat*," Mrs. García added.

Mr. García nodded, making his own notes in his tiny notebook. "Yes, it is all about the rice. Perfect rice texture— the *socarrat*—always the challenge."

Isabel smiled at him and whispered to me, "Wait till we got back home. I am sure my dad is inspired. He will break out his paella pan within a week."

I peeked over his shoulder and saw his evolving paella recipe—I was excited by the idea that we'd still have incredible Spanish paellas even after we left Spain!

Chapter 8

Surprise in Seville

Traveling to Seville was definitely bittersweet. I was excited to see the city and to see my parents, but I knew it meant we only had a few more days left in Spain.

My parents seemed relaxed and rested. They hugged us nonstop—whenever we were within arm's length, they were pulling us in for hugs.

Nic and Ryan immediately did the guy thing, boxing with my dad when they saw him. I will never understand how guys show affection. My dad took a few punches, but in the end, he bear-hugged them till they gave up.

Isabel and her family were staying with some friends on the outskirts of the city, but my family stayed in the heart of town in a hotel near the Seville Cathedral. Our room had a great view of the skyline, but I suddenly felt like a tourist; I was already missing the family and food in Colmenarejo.

We unpacked and did a whirlwind tour of the Seville Cathedral. I was surprised to learn that the church used to be a mosque. They started building it in the 1400s—and took centuries to finish!

We ended our tour in the royal chapel and walked down into the crypt. After seeing some of the tombs and spookier religious artifacts, I shivered and said to Mom, "I don't think I can tour or read any more about all the crypts and tombs—it gives me goosebumps."

Ryan hooted, "Crypts are the coolest part of the tours!"

I scrambled outside and took a big gulp of the fresh air. I was excited to see the Garcías, but as soon as they appeared, I thought maybe I should have taken my chances down in the crypts—they immediately warned us we were in for a long walk to the Ramón Sánchez-Pizjuán Stadium, and the sun here in Seville was just as intense as in Madrid. Mr. and Mrs. García had apparently promised the kids they would try and get a tour through the famous soccer stadium.

As we went along, the grown-ups kept on pointing out tourist sites and planning our next move. Quietly, Isabel and I slipped toward the back of the group.

Once I was positive no one could overhear, I whispered, "Were you able to ask your mom about the things we

found in the satchel?"

"No—she's been brushing me off nonstop. Anytime I bring up anything about our trip to Segovia or ask her anything about our family history, she says, 'Don't worry; just enjoy yourself.'" Isabel rolled her eyes and mimicked her mom pretty flawlessly.

I wanted to ask more, but after what seemed like hours of walking, we finally saw the enormous stadium come into view—it looked like it was a whole city block long! It was also covered in signs, and when Mr. García read them, his huge smile flipped all the way upside down.

"I am so sorry, kids—the entire stadium is closed for renovations! We can't even get tickets to tour the trophy room or the player's tunnel," he announced sadly.

The disappointment hit Guille, Nino, Isabel, and Ryan like a brick wall. Nino, who had been whining about the long walk the entire way, cried out, "But I wanted to run out the player's tunnel with Isabel, like a pro soccer—I mean pro fútbol—player!"

Before Nino could take it any further, Mrs. García quickly stepped in to bandage the situation. "That doesn't mean there aren't soccer shops and vendors. I bet they have some Sevilla FC historical shops too!"

We worked our way around the stadium and found a

bookstore that, sure enough, had all things soccer, including an entire wall dedicated to Sevilla FC soccer stuff—balls, hats, shirts, shorts, and other random trinkets with "Sevilla FC" scrawled all over them. There was also a bunch of stuff for another team, Real Betis Balompié, which was apparently also based here.

Tennis is my sport, I thought, *but the fútbol vibe here is real.*

I didn't know anything about either team, and Isabel was a huge Real Madrid fan, so we were both done browsing this section pretty quickly. Luckily, we spotted an alcove at the end of the wall that was brightly lit but pretty small; we made our way down into the alcove and saw that there was lots of stuff for other soccer teams, like Real Madrid and FC Barcelona.

Isabel picked up a soccer book and started flipping through it. She was mumbling to herself just loud enough that I could hear her reading: "Sevilla FC was founded in 1905, and at the time, mirrored the region and the culture of its people. This is similar to other fútbol clubs thought to have formed around the same time, like Real Club Recreativo de Huelva." She gasped, "Ruby, look—here is that word, Huelva! We heard my cousin yell it out during our fútbol game, too, and it's been bugging me ever since. Remember, the word I thought might be 'Huva' from the note? I wonder if I just wasn't able to decipher the handwriting well enough . . ."

She continued reading, but louder now and more furiously. "Around 1889, miners working in Huelva started playing fútbol; eventually, this led to the official formation of Club Recreativo de Huelva. They claim to be the first official fútbol club in Spain, but there is ongoing controversy about this point; other clubs claim they were formed by workers in a similar way, but even earlier."

Isabel looked up at me. "This is what Diego and Mateo were arguing about when we were about to eat the paellas!"

I looked at Isabel with eyes wide open, but I still didn't understand. "What would that have to do with the note we found?" I asked.

"Don't really know, but we definitely have to find out!" she cried and then added, "We're definitely buying this book! A history book, of all things. My mom will never let me live this down!"

Mrs. García found us at the register, but after looking at the book briefly, she just said, "We could all probably use a little snack right about now."

Isabel quickly found a fruit smoothie vendor who had any kind of fruit you could imagine in colorful cups. Ryan, Nino, Isabel, and I all got different flavors so we could sample as many as possible. The grown-ups found a booth selling olive kabobs with garlic and meats. Nic and Guille had both.

"If we can't remember whether we ate lunch or not, we just keep eating," joked Guille.

"Yeah, I just eat if I am hungry—which is most of the time. Seriously." Nic shrugged.

Chapter 9

Cook-Off Competition

After our whirlwind tour of Seville, I was excited to bring my parents back to Madrid and show them all of the spots I'd rated in my journal as "must-see"—or, more accurately, "must-eat!" Our excitement, however, was dulled by the long and boring train ride to Madrid. The parents enjoyed the scenic fields and rolling hills, but the rest of us only found comfort in the food cart.

Once we had settled back into the Garcías' Madrid apartment, one of our very first stops, of course, had to be the tías. They were just as warm and welcoming to my parents as they'd been to all of us, and they were excited to hear about our trip to Seville and the outskirts of Madrid.

As we covered the foods sampled in Seville, Ryan made another *Sliced* joke, and Tía Carla said, "*Los niños, hablan y se burlan mucho de estos concursos de cocina que hacen, pero no entiendo qué son 'Rebanadas' y porqué los pequeños siguen haciendo señales con las manos en un movimiento de 'parada?'*"

Mrs. García translated: "You children talk and tease much about cooking competitions, but she doesn't understand what '*Sliced*' is and why you keep signaling 'stop' with your hands."

Isabel giggled. "It isn't a stop signal. It is a slice—like cutting something with a knife? In this case, it would be cutting someone from a cooking competition."

Isabel quickly started sorting through her phone to find some clips, and as everyone gathered around to watch the little *Sliced* cooks compete, Nino stood on a chair and asserted, "We are foodies."

"I am the Fantastic Foo of eating," Ryan said, pointing proudly to his chest, "but Ruby is the Fantastic Foo of cooking!"

Nic nodded. "It's true—well, Ryan and I are still competing for the title in eating. But Ruby is a genius in the kitchen."

The looks on Mom and Dad's faces were priceless. I was a little shocked myself as I realized how much closer the trip to Spain had made me to my own siblings. I always knew my brothers loved my cooking—but a few weeks ago, I could have sworn they were incapable of complimenting me directly! I tried to conceal my smile so my mom wouldn't know just how right she'd been!

"What is your most impressive dish or favorite food?" Tía Lorena asked.

I searched my mental recipes before definitively stating, "*Lop chung.*"

At first, the words baffled everyone. I tried to explain, using "sausage" and "chorizo" several times, but they still didn't get it.

Isabel translated, "*Salciccia*. No, Tía, it's not blood sausage. *Lop chung* doesn't have blood in it—it's just pork—pig, like oink-oink."

Everyone smiled. "Oh, *cerdo-cerdo*," all the tías said in Spanish.

"Well, you have seen how much we Spaniards appreciate all things pig!" Tía Lorena exclaimed. "Surely, you would not leave our country before you show us a new way to eat this! Will you compete this *Sliced* for us?"

"Oh! I would love to cook for you! This is my Gong Gong's recipe, but I'm always trying to get better at it. It's just . . . well, I need Chinese sausages," I said, trying to think if I had sampled any Spanish sausages I could substitute.

Tía Carla clapped her hands excitedly. "*¡Esto no es problema! Hay varios mercados de chino cerca de la Plaza de*

España. ¡¿Apuesto a que tienen tu salchicha de cerdo ahí?!"

Mrs. García translated: "She said that's not a problem! There are several *mercados de chino*, Chinese markets, near the Plaza de España. They probably have Ruby's sausage."

The tías scurried around and arranged to send Aurelia, Isabel, and me to pick up the sausage. Before I knew what had happened, I'd been whisked away into the kitchen, and the contest was on!

Ryan and Nino insisted on officiating. It usually would have driven me crazy to have them underfoot in the kitchen, but I wasn't about to ruin the fun, frantic party atmosphere!

Isabel and I lined up at the counter, and Ryan announced, "The rules are there aren't rules, but the main ingredients are: eggs and sausage."

Gong Gong's Steamed Eggs

Total: 1 hour   Prep: 15 minutes
Cook: 35-45 minutes   Yield: 4 servings

Ingredients

✓ 8 eggs

✓ 2 or 3 lop chung (Chinese sausage links)

✓ 2 scallions or green onions

✓ 8 tablespoons of water or ½ cup of water (Note: 1 tablespoon of water per egg)

Directions

1. Crack 8 eggs into a bowl.
2. Whisk or beat eggs till well blended in the bowl. Set aside.
3. Rinse scallions or green onions under water.
4. Using either a green onion slicer or a knife, cut scallions thinly, about ½–1 inch in length.
5. Slice lop chung diagonally and thinly (optional: cut off ends of lop chung and remove casings).
6. Add water to the bottom of your steamer. Turn heat to medium.
7. Evenly sprinkle your sliced lop chung and the sliced scallions along the bottom of a 9-inch pie pan.
8. Add ½ cup water to your egg mixture. Whisk or beat egg mixture till well blended.
9. Pour egg mixture gently into the 9-inch pie pan.
10. Turn heat to medium low. Gently place pie pan into steamer and cover.
11. Periodically check that eggs are cooking on low and have a clean custard-like texture. If you notice bubbling, turn the heat lower.
12. After 30–35 minutes, turn heat up to simmer to finish cooking egg.

*Optional dipping sauce: Either oyster sauce or infused soy sauce.

*Best served over rice. Get your plated foodie photo, then enjoy!

87

ADVENTURE #2

Tortilla de Patatas a la Gallega

Total: 90 minutes   Prep: 45 minutes

Cook: 45 minutes   Yield: 4 servings

Ingredients

- ✓ 3 medium yellow/gold potatoes (choose potatoes similar in size)
- ✓ 1 medium onion
- ✓ 3 whole eggs
- ✓ ¼ teaspoon smoked sweet paprika
- ✓ ¼ cup of ground chorizo
- ✓ Salt to taste
- ✓ Olive oil (1½ cups)
- ✓ Juice of one tomato, freshly squeezed and any seeds strained
- ✓ Optional: use mandolin

Directions

Prepare the onions, potatoes, eggs and chorizo:

1. Crumble and brown the chorizo in a sauté pan (7–8 minutes on medium-high heat), remove from the pan when done, and allow to cool for 15 minutes. Set aside.
2. Beat the eggs in a large mixing bowl (needs to be large enough to add potato slices to the eggs later), just enough to where they have a little foam after beating. Add the juice from the tomato. Add the cooked chorizo and the sweet paprika. Mix the ingredients together, then set aside.
3. Peel the potatoes, and either manually slice them into thin slices, or use a mandolin. If using a mandolin, aim for ⅛-inch slices (thinner than this and they may cook too fast).
4. Slice the onion into thin slices (you can also use the mandolin for this and get the same ⅛-inch slice!).
5. Sprinkle the potatoes lightly with some salt.

88

Fry the onion and potatoes:

1. You want to fry the potatoes in a single layer if possible (not stacking the potatoes on top of each other) so that they cook evenly and quickly. You may want to split the potatoes into two batches to make things easier. Don't brown them—they should be tender but not overdone.
2. The onion can be done all at once with the first batch of potatoes or split into two batches just like the potatoes.
3. Heat the olive oil in a large sauté pan on high heat.
4. Add the sliced onion first, and sauté for 1–2 minutes.
5. Add the potatoes in a single layer, and cover with the oil.
6. Reduce heat to medium, and sprinkle the potatoes with a little more salt.
7. Cook the potatoes until they are just soft (about 5–6 minutes); do not brown them or completely fry them. Flip them once during cooking with a spatula.
8. Remove the potatoes and onions to a colander; reserve the oil in the sauté pan for the next batch of onions/potatoes if needed. If done, then reserve ¼ cup of the oil for the next steps.
9. Allow the potatoes and onions to cool in the colander 5–10 minutes.

Make the tortilla:

1. Add the potatoes and onions to the egg and chorizo mixture in the large bowl.
2. Turn the mixture gently with a soft spatula. The potato mixture should be coated with the egg mixture (but should not be drowned in it).
3. Let the mixture sit 15–20 minutes.
4. Heat a small sauté pan (6–8-inch pan for small tortillas) on high heat with 2–3 tablespoons of the olive oil you reserved from frying the potatoes.
5. When hot, add the potato-egg-chorizo mixture (if you are

89

making two smaller tortillas, then use half the mixture). Even out the mixture in the sauté pan with a soft spatula, and reduce heat to medium. Cook for 3–5 minutes.

6. Get ready to flip the tortilla. To do this, use your soft spatula to gently separate the tortilla from the side of the sauté pan (when doing this, you should not see the liquid egg mixture pouring out from the sides—if you do, cook another 1–2 minutes before flipping).

7. Using a plate slightly larger than the sauté pan, flip the tortilla quickly onto the plate.

8. Add an additional tablespoon of reserved olive oil to the sauté pan, and gently slide the tortilla from the plate back into the sauté pan (so that the uncooked side is now facing down in the pan).

9. Cook uncovered for another 3–4 minutes on medium heat.

10. Round out the tortilla against the sides with the soft spatula again. You can flip twice more now to solidify the shape of the tortilla—it should keep its form so that flipping is easy—but don't overcook!

11. Flip a final time onto your serving dish. Can be served hot or refrigerated (can be served at room temperature at another time, without reheating).

I immediately turned the heat on to simmer for my steamed eggs with *lop chung*. I could hear Gong Gong's voice in my head: *the temperature is very important.* Starting his recipe, I heard his voice again: *if your knife is dull, then just don't use it. Get another knife.* I held the base of my blade carefully and sliced away from myself, rhythmically, like they showed us during cooking camp. The *lop chung* package looked like the brand I usually bought, but now that I was cutting it thinly and at an angle, I knew it wasn't the same. I just hoped it tasted as good as the brand I used at home. I put my knife down and knocked twice (just in case) on the wooden cutting board.

Meanwhile, I could see Isabel starting her own recipe—her family's *tortilla a la Gallega con chorizo*. We were both getting some help from our families, which felt like cheating, but we were all having such a good time that it didn't matter. I stood in amazement as Isabel gently and very carefully used the mandolin for her potatoes. We heard Mrs. García say, "Sliced: Ancestral Amazing Edition," which made us smile. So extra, but extra didn't feel too bad in the heat of kitchen competition!

Finally, everyone congregated around the table, where Tía Paula had laid out little plates and forks. Isabel and I presented our plated dishes on the table, and everyone laughed as we danced around with the leftover sausages in our hands as if we were boxing.

Ryan declared, "Let the challenge begin: *lop chung* versus *chorizo*!" Nino translated, and the families lined up to take their plates.

"I am sorry, Ruby, but your dish, although colorful with the green onions, has to be cut because you added vegetables. According to my list, vegetables are not allowed," Ryan exclaimed, pretending to hold a piece of paper and then making a "sliced" motion with his arm and moving my plate to the side.

Tía Paula looked confused, pushed away her own sample of my dish, and asked, "*Qué pasa, qué haces?*"

Isabel explained that Ryan was joking, of course—that because he doesn't like vegetables, he sliced his sister from the competition. "*Un Chiste* . . . hahaha . . . a joke."

Tía Paula laughed, saying, "*Chiste, Chiste, broma,*" and dug into my sample.

Nic made a face at Ryan, and Ryan actually looked guilty! He smiled apologetically to me as he pulled his own sample of *lop chung* back in front of him and dug in. "If anyone can make vegetables delicious, it is definitely Ruby. She could be one of the world's most famous chefs someday!"

We all laughed, and my parents gave each other bewildered looks. I could almost see their minds going into overdrive: *Who are these children, and where are the real Ruby, Ryan, and Nic hiding?*

Sadly, I knew because of the bubbly texture that I'd flubbed the eggs, and the *lop chung* definitely wasn't as good as the brand I used at home. I'd known the odds of winning had been stacked against me like a lasagna casserole from the very beginning—people love the tastes that are most familiar to them, so most of my judges were already inclined toward the tortilla. Of course, none of the tías or Garcías wanted to discourage us, so they announced a tie; we were both winners.

After the contest, the tías decided to teach us all a Spanish card game, Tute, which seemed similar to gin rummy except the card faces had actual pictures of cups, swords, clubs, and coins. After playing a few hands, I started to watch for everyone's "tells." Nic, always competitive, was very eager to learn the game, but Guille got a small sparkle in his eye whenever he was about to win and would shuffle the cards a few more times than usual. Nic, on the other hand, got a disconcerting grin on his face whenever he shuffled the cards and tossed them between his fingers, but his Cheshire grin mercifully disappeared whenever it became obvious that his adversary's fate was sealed, replaced by an easy-going and playful smile. Guille and Nic traded wins back and forth for a while before the true upset— Ryan was a natural, and wiped us all out several times in a row.

Everyone continued snacking during the card games, and it soon became obvious that my steamed egg plates had outlasted Isabel's empty tortilla plates; the chorizo had indeed won by home advantage, and I vowed to perfect my recipe before I pulled it out in competition again.

"Oh well," I said to Isabel. "It looks like you won."

"Don't be silly," said Isabel, patting me on the back. "Almost everyone ate all the *lop chung*. Don't forget, it was most of the tías and my brothers' first experience with real Chinese food, so I think that's a pretty good result. I know what will cheer you up! My mom told me we're going to my Tía Lorena's apartment tomorrow for our last day in Spain. She's promised to show us how to make flan!"

I sighed deeply and dramatically. "I guess I can force myself to eat flan."

We both smiled—of course my best friend knew how much I loved flan!

"Oh! I'm glad we're going back to Tía Lorena's—we need to replace the leather bag," I said, remembering the "borrowed" satchel. "Did you ever get a chance to ask your mom about their mysterious Segovia hotel lunch? Who their 'friend' was? Did you bring up the note? And what was that book your mom hid in her purse?"

"Whoa—one question at a time! I tried to ask Mom about Segovia, but she just said I didn't need to worry about it—that everything was fine and good. Since she really didn't want to say anything else, there wasn't any way to bring up the note without admitting we'd been snooping. So, that was the end of that. But I did do some more reading from the fútbol book. I definitely think 'Huva' was 'Huelva', since we found that old fútbol in the satchel! I hope Tía Lorena is able to tell me something good tomorrow—I really don't have enough yet for my extra credit." Isabel shook her head, looking a little sad but also a little pleased with her research.

I knew Isabel wished she'd learned more, and I was frustrated that these mysteries seemed destined to go unsolved. But we both looked at Tía Lorena and Mrs. García, laughing and chatting, and had to admit that we were all having a good time—all the stress had melted away in Segovia.

Finally, so late into the night that it felt like nearly morning, we all said our goodbyes and headed back to the Garcías' apartment. Tía Carla and Tía Paula loaded Ryan and Nino up with handfuls of marzipan candy for the short trip and made us all promise to visit them again soon.

Chapter 10

Mystery in Madrid

"Café solo, café con leche, *café cortado* or *café con hielo*, I will drink any coffee—except, of course, if it is *descafeinado,"* my dad bellowed as he wandered into the kitchen the next morning, still yawning and waking up.

Isabel laughed and raised an eyebrow at me. "Decaf . . . your dad is bilingual in dad jokes."

"I want to talk about some *huevos*. I am starving," Dad said.

"Dad, eggs are *not* a breakfast food. Not in Spain."

My dad looked at me, surprised. "No way, Ruby! I know I've only been here for a few days, but I've seen *huevos* on every menu!"

Isabel chimed in. "We have lots of eggs on our menus, sure—for lunch, dinner, and tapas!"

"I take my eggs with *chorizo* or *jamón*—no vegetables. Are potatoes vegetables? I like potatoes," Ryan said decisively.

Dad shook his head. "Everyone is a food critic, and I am just hungry. You know I enjoy a nice big breakfast! Suggestions?"

"Well, I know you've been having those hotel-style big breakfast buffets for tourists. But for locals, breakfast is a smaller meal. 'When in Madrid . . .'" I said, winking at Mom.

Mom smiled at me, and Dad whimpered, "Okay, but I have to eat something!"

"I know! I know!" roared Nino. "The *chocolatería*! *Churros* and *porras*! Please!" He begged.

Isabel, Guille, and Nino looked imploringly at their dad while my family and I just looked confused.

Nino quickly turned to rally Ryan, explaining, "*Porras* and *churros* are like donuts that you dip in real melted chocolate!"

Ryan squealed, "I love donuts! Please, Mom and Dad? We only have one more day to eat Spanish donuts—please?"

I chimed in. "I am sure the *churros* and *porras*—whichever one you choose—would be perfect dunked in a cup of coffee."

I winked at my mom, who replied, "You kids are relentless!"

Although it was unfair, we all ganged up to hurry the adults to the local *chocolatería*.

Mrs. García smiled and joined in. "I know it sounds excessive, fried donuts dipped in a cup of liquid chocolate, but they *are* a Madrid specialty."

I grinned. I couldn't wait to see my parents experience real Spanish hot chocolate—the thick, dark, soupy hot fudge I'd come to love during our trip.

★ ★ ★

After our breakfast at the *chocolatería*, we headed to Tía Lorena's apartment. Oddly, Tía Lorena immediately shooed everyone else out the door to go explore the city so that she and Aurelia could spend some time with just Isabel and me in the kitchen.

"Aurelia will be helping us to make the special *Tarta de Santiago*," Tía Lorena explained, "and I will be teaching you all to make flan, as promised."

Aurelia smiled. "I have heard much of Tía Lorena's flan; it is quite legendary. But she has never made it in all the years I have been with her."

"Why not, Tía?" Isabel asked.

Tía Lorena smiled, but it was a sad smile. "I . . . did not feel like making it for many years. But do not worry about that. Let's enjoy!"

Isabel rolled her eyes at me, and I shrugged. Adults were all so secretive!

Aurelia busied around, taking instruction from Tía Lorena about how to begin the caramel for flan. This recipe lived entirely inside Tía Lorena's head, but I saw a cookbook on the counter and stepped up to look. It was, of course, in Spanish, so Isabel came over to help me translate.

"Almond flour, sugar, eggs, orange, lemon, and vanilla," Isabel read off, looking confused. "This doesn't seem like flan . . ."

Tía Lorena laughed. "You are jumping ahead! This is for the *Tarta de Santiago*, a cake named after the apostle Saint James. No one knows for certain why it is named for him, but in Galicia, there is the Cathedral of Santiago de Compostela, where they believe Saint James' relics are located, so you would see this cake in every Galician bakery, delicately adorning every window with the Saint James Cross. Once we finish the flan, we will begin on this. This is my favorite."

Tarta de Santiago

Total: 1 hour   Prep: 20–25 minutes
Cook: 25–30 minutes   Yield: 8–10 servings

Ingredients:

- ✓ 7 egg yolks; 3-4 egg whites
- ✓ 1¼ cups of white sugar
- ✓ Zest of 1 small orange
- ✓ Zest of 1 lemon

- ✓ 2⅓ cups of Almond flour
- ✓ 1 tablespoon vanilla extract
- ✓ Powdered sugar for dusting
- ✓ 9-inch springform pan

Directions

1. Preheat oven to 350 degrees.
2. Butter the sides and bottom of the 9-inch springform pan.
3. Zest the whole lemon. Zest the whole small orange.
4. In a large mixing bowl, cream the egg yolks and sugar together by hand.
5. Once mixed well, add in almond flour, vanilla extract, and orange and lemon zest.
6. In mixer, beat egg whites to stiff peaks.
7. Gently fold in ¼ egg whites into the almond flour mix.
8. Then, add in the rest of the egg white mixture.
9. Bake for 20 minutes at 350 degrees Farenheit.
10. After 20 minutes, test with a toothpick. If it is dry, it is done.
11. Let cool for 30–50 minutes.
12. While the tart is cooling, cut out a stencil of the Saint James's Cross (you can easily locate a stencil online).
13. When the tart is cool, place the Saint James's Cross stencil on the center of the tart, and sprinkle the entire tart with powdered sugar. Then, lift off the stencil to reveal the shape of the cross.

*Share a photo and enjoy!

101

ADVENTURE #2

Just at that moment, we all heard something crackle on the stovetop.

"Oh no!" Tía Lorena said as Aurelia hurried to turn down the burner. "I was distracted, and I did not keep my eyes on the caramel."

Isabel and I looked inside the saucepan, which was now coated with burned, sugary shards.

Tía Lorena picked up the pot. "If you stir the sugar too much, it just crystallizes. You must lift the saucepan and gently swirl the caramel, keeping a low to medium heat. *Paciencia* until just *color de caramelos*. Just like you need *paciencia* for the flan itself: low and slow."

Flan

Total: 8-10 hours   Prep: 30-40 minutes
Cook: 9-10 hours (includes refrigeration time)   Yield: 5-6 servings

Ingredients

- ✓ ¼–½ teaspoon zest of one orange
- ✓ Zest of 1 lemon
- ✓ 2 large egg yolks
- ✓ 6 large whole eggs
- ✓ 3 cups of whole milk
- ✓ 2½ cups of sugar
- ✓ 1 small pinch of salt
- ✓ Two 7 inch x 4 ½–inch mini casserole bakeware dishes

- ✓ One 9–inch x 13–inch rectangular cakepan or roasting pan (You will place both mini casseroles inside the larger rectangular cakepan or roasting pan.)
- ✓ Stainless–steel saucepan, small
- ✓ Large bowl, preferably with a spout or lip for pouring
- ✓ Medium bowl

Directions

Caramelize the sugar

1. Add 2 tablespoons of water and 1 cup of sugar to a small, stainless–steel saucepan.
2. Turn heat to medium-low.
3. Do not stir. Be patient and watch. In about 15–20 minutes, the sugar will start to melt and crystallize along the sides of the pan. You should see parts of the sugar turn amber/brown color.
4. Once the sugar is melting and changing color, swirl the saucepan around gently to make sure the melting and browning is happening evenly. This should take about 30 minutes total from start to finish.

103

5. Once all the sugar is caramelized, quickly pour the caramel into the two mini casseroles and rotate the casseroles to coat the bottoms and sides. Do this quickly as the caramel will harden when taken off the heat.
6. Let caramel cool and harden in the mini casseroles.
7. When you are done with the caramel, fill a tea kettle or pot with water and bring to a boil, and preheat the oven to 325 degrees on bake.

Make the custard:

1. In a regular sized saucepan, add in ¾ cup sugar, the lemon zest, orange zest, salt, and whole milk. Heat to simmer.
2. Separately, in the medium bowl, add another ¾ cup sugar, the eggs, egg yolks, and cream together.
3. While your baking buddy continues to whisk the egg mixture in the medium bowl, pour the simmering milk from the saucepan into the medium bowl.
4. Gently pour the final mixture from the medium bowl into the large bowl with the spout through a fine sieve, strainer, or cheesecloth (remove and discard zest and foam).

Make the flan:

1. Place the two mini casserole dishes into the large cakepan or roasting pan.
2. Take the large bowl with the spout and carefully pour the strained custard mixture into the two caramel-coated mini casserole dishes. Fill to the top.
3. Fill the cakepan or roasting pan with the hot water from the tea kettle. The water should reach about halfway up the sides of the mini casserole dishes.
4. Bake for about 60 minutes. Check the flan with a toothpick. Continue to bake in 5-minute increments, checking the flan with

a toothpick in the center until it comes out clean.

5. Cool on a wire rack for about 45 minutes.

6. Refrigerate for at least 6–8 hours.

Flan presentation:

1. Use a knife along the sides of the flans to remove them from the mini casserole dishes.

2. Gently flip the mini casserole dish onto a flat plate.

3. Pour the extra caramel from the mini casserole dish over the top of the flan.

*Share your flan by taking a photo, then enjoy!

Tía Lorena shooed Isabel and me out of the kitchen while she and Aurelia tried to save the batch, promising that they would come get us when they were ready to get started again. Apparently, you needed two people for the recipe, one to swirl the other to whisk and pour the custard. Although I normally would have enjoyed the chance to see how to fix a recipe that had gone sideways, this was the perfect opportunity to restore the leather satchel to its spot in the storage room.

As we crept through the hallway, I laughed quietly. "Flan might not be my culinary calling. 'Low and slow' is exactly the direction my Gong Gong gives me for the steamed eggs, and you tasted how that turned out. Impatience is my curse."

Isabel smirked. "You are getting more superstitious every

day. Flan must be creamy and thick and melt in your mouth like warm chocolate molten cake. But if you're worried about the custard, you will absolutely love learning how to make the *Tarta de Santiago*. It is heavenly."

We stopped in our tracks when we noticed something different on the small table in the hallway. There was a notebook open that hadn't been there the last time we'd snuck through. I noticed it because it was old, but when Isabel got closer, she turned to me, her eyes wide.

"Ruby! This is the book from Segovia. The one my mom tried to hide from us in her purse!" She flipped quickly through the pages and looked puzzled. "This handwriting—doesn't it match the note from the satchel perfectly? Quick, grab it and double check," Isabel begged.

I dug through the satchel for the note, and Isabel grabbed the notebook. We sat them beside each other on the floor and leaned in close to look. Isabel was right! There were two sets of handwriting on the note, but one of them had very distinctive and unusual *a*'s and *r*'s, which matched the writing in the notebook perfectly.

Before Isabel and I could say anything more, Tía Lorena suddenly materialized right behind us.

"There you girls are! I was afraid Zorro got you!" she laughed. "I sent Aurelia out for more sugar and more ingredients . . ."

Isabel and I both spun around, and I knew we looked guilty—because we were. Tía Lorena's eyes shot toward the notebook and the leather satchel on the floor, and she gasped, visibly shocked. Isabel and I were frozen for a moment, and Zorro stared down at us, very disappointed, as Tía Lorena stumbled out of the hallway.

Isabel was the first to dash out to find her tía, but I ran closely behind her. Tía Lorena sat in a chair in the main room with a faraway look on her face and tears in her eyes. The trip to Spain had been so wonderful—but now we'd ruined it all!

"I'm so sorry," Isabel said, tears welling up in her own eyes. "We shouldn't have been snooping, Tía Lorena. It's just . . . well, we only visit once a year, and I was just looking to see what other beautiful things you have. We ended up in your storage room before we left for Segovia, and I borrowed your bag for our trip. We weren't stealing anything, I swear! I should have asked, but we were returning it."

I swallowed hard, knowing I needed to step in and take some responsibility too. I held the leather satchel out to Tía Lorena and volunteered, "We accidentally ripped the liner and found this note and a fútbol. If you have thread and a needle, I'd like to try and patch it up. I'll even stay out of the kitchen all day to do it!"

RUBY FOO

Tía Lorena gently took the bag and slowly read the note—suddenly, a subtle, small, pleasant smile appeared through her tears!

Kneeling down next to her, Isabel said softly, "I am so sorry, Tía Lorena. We never should have gone through your things or tried to read them. It's just . . . well, the handwriting in the note and the notebook are the same, and I was so curious to know who Rob was. I've been trying to learn more about our history for our entire trip, but even with all the Spanish history surrounding us, my own family is still a mystery to me."

"Oh, Issy, I . . . I . . ."

Tía Lorena covered her face with her hands and started crying harder, reaching for her handkerchief. Isabel looked like she wanted to sink further into the floor, and I couldn't help but wonder how furious both our moms would be when they returned for lunch.

Tía Lorena took her hands away from her face, and we could see she was still smiling through her tears. It was very confusing.

"Yes," she said, as though she'd just made up her mind about something. "Yes, it is the same handwriting. Yes, you should know about my husband, your Tío Roberto."

Isabel's eyes got wide. "I thought I had another tío, but I

never knew his name," she murmured.

"To explain who Roberto was, I must explain many things from my early life, Issy, and some of those thoughts are not happy or easy for me to even think of. Are you sure you would like to hear these things?" Tía Lorena asked haltingly.

Isabel nodded and squeezed my hand for comfort. I squeezed it back, glad I could be here for my best friend. Isabel's eyes beseeched her tía to continue.

Tía Lorena took a deep breath and began. "Well, okay. I am sure your parents told you about the terrible Spanish Civil War. From 1936 to 1939, brothers fought against each other, and close friends and neighbors turned into bitter enemies. More than half a million of my country's men, women, and children died, and the suffering touched us all.

"Though I was a young girl, I, like all Madrileños who were alive at that time, remember the hunger well. We lived on lentils and sweet potatoes. There was no meat, no rice, no fruit, and rarely milk and eggs. Just before the war ended, I remember that small loaves of bread floated from the sky, wrapped in the Spanish flag—the promise of how once the war was over, we would never be without bread again.

"Just as the war ended, though, there was a drought that lasted three years. Food, already so scarce, became tightly rationed. We could still rarely get meat, eggs, or milk; I remember many times when all I knew was the taste of chickpeas, sweet potatoes, pasta, and salted fish. Even water was hard to get in some places. We did not get enough to eat, and so many became so sick in ways that would haunt us for years to come. These were *los años del hambre*—the hunger years.

"When you asked me, Ruby, whether I had learned to bake bread from my mother when I was your age, I did not know how to answer. My mother, like many others, struggled to feed her family. She taught me to cook food without oil, tortillas without eggs, bread without wheat. She would send me and my brothers and sister out to the hillsides to collect wild herbs and grasses, thistles, acorns, orange and lemon rinds—anything to stretch our food further and make it taste better."

"I'm so sorry," I whispered, tears welling up in my eyes. "I had no idea."

Tía Lorena reached out and grasped my hand. "No, no. It is good to talk of these things. It is good to understand. Now you see another important reason why we in Spain treasure our food, why we make our meals so delicious, why we make them parties. I am so honored to be able to teach you our family recipes, our cultural cookbook, because it is our history."

She took a deep breath and continued, "I met a boy of my age when I was just a few years older than you two are

111

now. This was my Roberto, but he had to be sent away."

"Who sent him away? Where did he go?" Isabel asked, hungrily lapping up the information about her family.

Tía Lorena continued softly, "Every man spent a period of military service for their country, even when there was no war, even when they might not have agreed with all things the government was doing."

"Conscription—just like Prince Harry in England!" Isabel volunteered.

"Yes, like this." Tía Lorena agreed. "The Spanish Army is one of the oldest active armies in the world—it has existed since the reign of King Ferdinand and Queen Isabella, the same regents who funded Columbus's exploration of the Americas. Although all men do not have to join the army now, when your Tío Roberto was a young man, refusing would have put him in prison. Your Tío Roberto was an engineer, and he traveled to every region and saw what made each of them special and wonderful. He dreamed of creating spaces where all Spaniards could live together peacefully and enjoy what made us all countrymen together while sharing what made us all unique. This book of notes and maps was one he carried to each region, documenting his travels and everything he learned. Although he saw the beauty in each part of the country, he held a special love in his heart for Andalusía. It holds some of the great treasures of Spain—the Alhambra in Granada, the gothic cathedral in Sevilla, and many others. It also holds many smaller towns, including Huelva in the northwest part of la Costa de la Luz, two to three hours from Sevilla."

"'Seville' and 'Huelva' are both on the note we found in the bag!" I said excitedly.

"Yes—fútbol is a common tie for all Spaniards, and there was a great deal of fútbol in Sevilla and Huelva. Tío Roberto visited many times, and he met men who belonged to the Huelva Club, one of the country's first fútbol clubs, founded in about 1889. Huelva is home to a great mine, Rio Tinto, once owned by the British, and the British miners brought the game to this country with them. At first, the club was comprised mostly of British players, but the Spanish soon began playing, too."

"Did Tío Roberto join the club in Huelva?" Isabel asked, clearly holding her breath.

Tía Lorena smiled, imagining her husband when they were young. "No, though I am sure he wished he was a player for the team. From the moment he met them, he made a mission to meet every fútbol club in every place that the military sent him. He made friends at every stop and sent me letters reporting on what he learned from each of them. You have just come back from Sevilla—Issy, surely you know Sevilla FC, the main rivals of Real Betis, yes?"

Issy nodded her head.

"Barcelona is part of Catalonia, and the Catalonians, who wanted independence from Spain, were not allowed by the government of the time to speak their own language anywhere but one place: the fútbol grounds. Your Tío Roberto loved to meet all the people and hear them speak the languages of their homes and to hear what they most easily expressed in their own tongues. Whenever he was on leave, he would take me to meet the people that he had met through his mission. In this way, we traveled the country together and learned how all people lived."

I looked at Isabel, astonished. She was glowing brightly, realizing that her love for soccer was even more important to her family and her history than she had previously known.

"Your Tío Roberto saw so much and was loved by so many in such a short time. He passed when we were still quite young—younger than your own parents," Tía Lorena said softly. "Roberto was back in Huelva visiting with his friends from the club when he got sick. He was often sick because he did not get enough to eat when he was still a child and growing, and that can make your body weak, no matter how tall you get. The day I got the message that he was gone was so sad for me that I was unable to speak of it. Our family, to be kind to me, has rarely brought up his memory again until now."

"Why can you speak of him now?" Isabel asked softly. "Why was the notebook out on the table if it causes you so much pain?"

"I can speak now because I think Tío Roberto is calling on me to tell his story, or our story, to the family," Tía Lorena said. "Just a few months ago, I received a message from an American girl, Ms. Martinez, who was cleaning out her great-grandparents' apartment in Huelva. When she saw Tío Roberto's notebook, which must have been left behind when he passed so suddenly, she decided to find me and return it. I asked your mother to accompany me to Segovia to retrieve it, as I did not want to miss a word in translation and ensure we had perfect communication. It was a twist of fate that you discovered the note and the fútbol in the satchel the same day—almost magical. That is why we are celebrating with Roberto's favorite, my flan, which I have not made since he passed. And we will serve it side by side with my favorite dessert, Tarta de Santiago."

In my mind, I pumped my fist up the air—superstition for the win! I'd be sure to remind Isabel of this example of a magical coincidence the next time she laughed at me for my superstitious ways. Not today, obviously!

"What does the note say?" I asked.

"Let's see it again with my glasses, let's see here . . . 'If

Roberto keeps practicing fútbol every day, then he will, of course, get better and feel luckier.'"

I smiled. "That sounds like a Chinese fortune cookie!"

Tía Lorena and Isabel both laughed and hugged each other, and we heard Aurelia unlock the door. We all jumped up, and Isabel and I went to go help her with the bags as Tía Lorena dried her eyes.

★ ★ ★

By the time our families were pulled back to Tía Lorena's apartment, we could tell by the scents and vision of caramel clouds for lunch that the *tarta* was coming out of the oven, and the flan had nearly finished its hour of sitting in the fridge. Tía Lorena was happily transcribing the recipes for both desserts to Isabel and me, pausing every so often to ask us for the English translation of one word or another.

Although Tía Lorena was in quite high spirits, Mrs. García could tell something had changed. She pulled Isabel and me aside at the first opportunity and said suspiciously, "Tía Lorena seems a little emotional . . ."

Isabel smiled mysteriously at her mother, and they went to go speak quietly in Zorro's hallway. Tía Lorena had already promised Isabel that she would share every detail that she knew of their family history with her—every letter, every story—and that Isabel could take the reins and be the family historian.

An hour later, Aurelia announced, "*El flan y la tarta están listas!*"

Isabel took a huge forkful of the flan. "Yummm! This is like eating the thickest, creamiest caramel."

I took a bite and sighed.

Mr. García was confused. "What's wrong? You don't like it?"

I shook my head. "Of course, I love it, but it has the velvety consistency that I should have had for my steamed eggs! A thick, creamy, custard–like consistency!"

"Stop thinking about the contest, and just enjoy your desserts," Nic commanded.

With a forkful of *Tarta de Santiago*, I said, "I do love dessert! This cake is so moist. And, the almond citrus flavor balances perfectly on my tongue!"

Isabel chimed in. "The smell, or should I say the citrus fragrance, is dreamy delicious!"

I smiled and corrected her. "You mean Foolicious!"

Chapter 11

Passage to the New World

Isabel had been correct—her dad was so inspired and eager to test out his new theory around perfecting his paella rice that the airplane had barely touched down back in the US before he invited all of us over for a big, Spanish-style lunch. My parents tried to decline, since the Garcías had already been such generous hosts in Spain. They told him that Gong Gong was coming over to hear about our trip, but Mrs. García wouldn't accept any excuse.

"Bring him along! I am going to miss all the big family meals we've been having—let's have one more to cap off our trip to Spain! I just need to make one quick stop first to pick up an air fryer. I simply must test Tía Carla's ancestral amazing ham and olive *croqueta* recipe for myself."

I caught Isabel's eye, smiling, and she made a face. I knew we were both thinking the same thing—*so extra*. But if anyone knew anything about being extra about food, it was us. Plus, who could complain about more of those *croquetas!*

Just a few hours later, Isabel and I sat together on her

deck. Around the side of the house, we could hear Nino, Ryan, and Nic teaching Gong Gong how to play soccer in the Spanish style—very, very loudly! The aroma from Mrs. García's homemade *croquetas* mixed with the aroma of the rice and chicken stock cooking in the new and hastily constructed paella pit in the backyard. We watched Isabel's dad standing with Guille, both with their aprons on, looking as serious and fully engaged as their Spanish cousins about the paella. My mouth was watering—I had gotten a good look at the recipe Mr. García had made from all the notes he'd taken in Spain, and it looked incredible!

LOBSTERS

MUSSELS

SHRIMP

Olive Oil

CHICKEN

STEWED Tomatoes

SMOKED PAPRIKA

JUDION BEANS
EXTRA QUALITY

GRILLED
Piquillo Peppers
IN WATER

ESPECIAL
PAELLA

Seafood
Culinary
Stock

ARROZ "CALASPARRA"
Traditional Paella Rice

Paella

Total: 1¾ hours (will be longer with homemade ingredients) Prep: 1 hour
Cook: 45 minutes   Yield: 6 servings

Ingredients

- ✓ 2 cups of short grain rice (e.g., *bomba, calasparra*) (Note that if using more rice, you will need to change the amount of stock you use.)
- ✓ 1½ pounds boneless chicken thighs
- ✓ ½ pound raw shrimp, peeled and deveined
- ✓ One lobster tail per person, thawed if frozen
- ✓ ½ pound mussels
- ✓ ½ pound littleneck clams
- ✓ ½ teaspoon smoked sweet paprika
- ✓ Fresh thyme, 2–3 sprigs
- ✓ Fresh rosemary, 2–3 sprigs
- ✓ Fresh parsley
- ✓ Juice of 1 lemon
- ✓ Salt and pepper to taste
- ✓ ½ teaspoon saffron, toasted lightly and pulverized
- ✓ ½ cup of piquillo peppers, sliced
- ✓ ½ cup canned navy beans, liquid strained
- ✓ Olive oil
- ✓ Sofrito—a pureed tomato, garlic, and onion base (*options: use store bought, or see www.rubyfookitchen.com for homemade suggestion)
- ✓ 8–12 cups of chicken or seafood stock (*options: same as above; you should have some extra stock when done)
- ✓ 15-inch paella pan

Directions

1. Prepare the stock and ingredients.
2. Heat the stock in a large stock pot, and bring to simmer. Keep

121

hot while the paella is being prepared.

3. Wash and dry the chicken, and salt and pepper generously.
4. Wash/scrub the mussels and clams.
5. Peel and devein the shrimp.
6. Lightly toast the saffron in some tin foil until you smell its aroma (toasts quickly so be careful). Then pulverize/press with the back of a spoon, or use a mortar and pestle.
7. Preheat the oven on bake to 350 (optional; see below).

Make the paella:

1. The entire cooking process can be done on the stove top or an outdoor burner. Alternatively, after the stock is added, the paella can be placed inside an oven to cook. This recipe assumes use of the stove top. Make sure to use a large, wooden spoon (not metal) when mixing any ingredients.
2. On the stove top, heat the olive oil in the center of the paella pan on high heat.
3. Reduce the heat to medium, and add the chicken to the center of the pan with rosemary and thyme sprigs. Brown for about 5 minutes, turning liberally, then push the chicken to the outside of the pan, where it is cooler.
4. Add the shrimp in the center of the pan, add the juice of one lemon, and sauté quickly for 1–2 minutes until just turning pink. Remove from the paella pan onto a warm plate, and set aside.
5. Add the lobster tails to the center of the pan and sauté briefly to warm them through, about 2 minutes. Do not cook them through as they will be steamed later. Remove the tails on the warm plate with the shrimp and set aside.
6. Add the sofrito and simmer in the center of the pan for 5 minutes. Push toward the side of the pan, but do not mix with the chicken.
7. Add the piquillo peppers to the center of the pan, sauté for 2–3 minutes, and push out to the sides of the pan with the sofrito.
8. Add 5–6 tablespoons of additional olive oil to the center of the pan.

9. When the oil is hot, add the rice, and gently coat the rice in the oil over medium heat, folding the rice into the oil, taking care not to damage the rice. Do this with a wooden spoon for about 3–4 minutes.

10. Add the smoked sweet paprika and fold into the rice and oil gently.

11. Bring the sofrito and piquillo peppers into the rice mixture, and mix together gently. Cook for an additional 1–2 minutes.

12. Spread out the rice across the pan, and mix with the chicken.

13. Distribute the beans across the paella.

14. Add 6–7 cups of the stock slowly across the pan such that the rice and other ingredients are covered, and add in the saffron (you can add the saffron directly to the stock before pouring). The amount of stock you use at this point will vary; take care not to drown the rice (the stock should just cover the rice). Keep the heat on low-medium, and from this point on, do not stir the rice.

15. Simmer for 10 minutes, then bury the shrimp, clams, and mussels in the rice. Place the lobster tails decoratively on top of the rice (don't push them into the rice) to steam them. You can use a small piece of tin foil to loosely cover each tail to help them steam evenly (but don't put the foil on the rice).

16. At this point, you can choose to continue on the stove top or place the paella in the oven (using the stove top will ensure the lobster continues to steam nicely). If using the oven, place the paella in the oven for approximately 15 minutes. Otherwise, simmer on the stove top another 7–8 minutes. Verify that the rice is cooked through and that the desired consistency is achieved. Also make sure the clams and mussels have opened (discard any that didn't open later), and check that the lobsters are bright red in color.

17. When the rice is cooked, turn the stove top burner on high and cook the paella for another 2–3 minutes to crust the bottom layer of the rice and yield the *socarrat* (you may smell a light burning).

18. Remove from the heat and let stand for at least 15 minutes. Garnish with parsley before serving.

"Thanks again for taking me to Spain, Isabel. Meeting your family was amazing," I said, watching the gray squirrels dash up the trees and remembering the small lizards in Segovia. Now that I thought about it, I couldn't remember seeing a single gray squirrel anywhere in Spain!

"You've thanked me already so many times, Ruby. I should be thanking you. You were really patient and understanding around the whole Tío Roberto and Tía Lorena thing and spending so much time with my family and yours—and you even played fútbol! At least you got to experience some amazing food!" Isabel said, smiling broadly and flipping her ponytail off her neck.

I smiled back and picked up the ancient soccer ball that Tía Lorena had gifted to Isabel as we'd left Madrid, tossing it lightly to my best friend. "Now, I get it! Really. I didn't get it when we were sitting on the grass in Segovia, but now I understand why the notebook and soccer ball are so important to you."

Isabel hugged the soccer ball tightly with tears in her eyes. "I don't even know if I fully 'got it' before. I've always loved fútbol, but I just feel even more connected to it now, or like I understand my identity with it better. Like I'm channeling my Spanish ancestors, like it's in my blood. Even more than Tío Roberto's story, just listening to my cousins in Spain, where they know the fútbol rivalries so well . . .

I mean, you have all your customs, like your red envelopes and new year's traditions. I feel like fútbol is my tradition, part of my roots. How cool is it that my great tío spent so much time and gave so much attention to Recreativo de Huelva, one of the founding clubs of all of Spanish fútbol?"

"You see? Ancestral amazing!" Mrs. García crowed.

"Mom! How long have you been standing there?" Isabel shouted. She was already a little sore that her mom had managed to drag the entire story of Tío Roberto out of her in Tía Lorena's apartment hallway with Zorro sitting in judgment.

"Oh honey, not long. Well, long enough. I was thinking the same thing as you—I love going back to Spain and connecting with our roots, our history. I learn more about myself and my family around every corner, in every interaction, and with every dish," Mrs. García replied, placing the plate of crispy *croquetas* in front of us. "Do you know that the city of Huelva is also where Columbus organized his voyage to the New World? There are still replicas of his ships there. It is surreal to think that Tío Roberto may have been standing on the exact ground Columbus did at almost the exact moment that your abuelo decided to begin his journey to America—do you realize he was the first and only of his six siblings to leave Spain?"

Isabel rolled her eyes. "Mom, that is extra."

Mrs. García's expression changed from animated to scowling when she realized that "extra" was not a compliment. She quickly turned her back and trudged back inside the house.

"Hey, you never told me if your mom punished you for the satchel and notebook snooping," I said.

"Nope, I didn't get in trouble. She actually apologized for being so snappish with me, and she was so excited to read my extra credit assignment before I emailed it to Mrs. Zecker! My mom was relieved that everything was resolved with Tía Lorena. Mom was stressed because Tía Lorena asked her to help with getting the notebook, but she didn't want to tell the whole family because Tía Lorena has never wanted to talk about Tío Roberto. Plus, out of everyone in Spain, Tía Lorena asked my mom to help her! Mom was so afraid something would go wrong and Tía Lorena would be disappointed, but keeping secrets from my dad and all of us was tough when she was constantly getting calls and messages from Ms. Martinez," Isabel explained.

"At least Ms. Martinez wasn't a Spanish STEM tutor!" I laughed.

"But Mom would not be a very good time-traveling spy," Isabel joked.

"Oh, I don't know . . ." I said, pretending to think about it. "She could be . . . ancestral amazing!"

We both cracked up.

"Seriously, though, your mom wasn't that extra."

Isabel sighed. "I know, but I feel like she listens in on *every* conversation."

I rolled my eyes. "Please, my mom is way worse than your mom. She has so many restrictions on my phone, laptop, and tablet."

"It's weird, right? Like, both of our families keep all these secrets we're just starting to find, and we're not even allowed to have a private conversation," Isabel said.

"You're right. I wonder what other mysteries are floating out there . . ." I said, as we both bit into another perfectly sized *croqueta*.

★ ★ ★

It was nearly six-thirty in the evening by the time we finished Mr. García's homecoming paella attempt; not only was it a great success, but just like that, we were back in sync with dinner at dinner time. Isabel and our parents took Gong Gong's place in the soccer games, and my grandfather and I sat back and watched.

"Ryan is much better at soccer than Nic," Gong Gong observed.

It was true. Nic's gangly height and long gait enabled

him to outpace us all on the tennis court, but Ryan's speed and low center of gravity were winning out here. I smiled, happy that my baby brother was finding things he was the best at now each and every day.

Gong Gong asked me questions about the trip, and I told him everything we'd seen and eaten.

"Speaking of eating," he said, "it was nice of your friends to invite me over, but what was that I ate? Pay-ya?"

I laughed, "Almost, Gong Gong—it's pronounced *pie-eh-yah*. Get it?"

He shook his head. "No, but I liked the sausage."

"Speaking of sausage . . ." I took a deep breath and admitted to my *lop chung* failure.

After hearing the story, Gong Gong looked confused. "The family made you compete for food?" Gong Gong asked.

I laughed. "No, Gong Gong; we'd just been talking about *Sliced Junior*—"

Gong Gong interrupted with, "Sliced who?" in such a loud, booming voice that it attracted Ryan's attention as he ran inside to get a drink of water. We both giggled.

"Not 'who.' It's a show, Gong Gong!" Ryan shouted out.

Gong Gong replied, "Show me what?"

Ryan giggled again and ran back to the soccer game.

"It's a show on TV; everyone gets a basket of ingredients they have to use to cook whatever they can dream up. In the end, the judges decide who made the best dish, and who gets 'sliced'—get it?"

Gong Gong replied, "Yeah, yeah, sure. Why don't you use something with lemon and meringue and I can judge."

I chuckled. "Gong Gong, you can't just call out ingredients like lemon and meringue. We all know lemon meringue pie is your favorite. Plus, I don't even have anyone to compete against right now!"

"Hm. Maybe we can do something about that. But you won with my steamed egg recipe?"

I hung my head in shame. "My eggs just didn't have that velvety texture yours always do."

"It isn't easy to get that silky texture. You have to be patient and steam on low and slow. You know how you are—always rushed. So, when you found out you lost, did you get *steamed*? Get it? That's a pun. You like puns."

I smiled. "I do like puns, Gong Gong. Thanks for trying."

"Well, if you're not too tired out, I think you should start planning another trip."

"Oh, right; Mom told me!"

Gong Gong looked more grumpy than usual. "Oh, she did, did she?"

"Yeah! An archaeological dig in Boston—that's exciting," I said, trying to figure out what I'd said wrong. "Ryan wants to do a big lobster taste test while we're there."

Gong Gong's face relaxed, and he grinned. "Oh, yes, well, that will be quite something. But I have a bigger surprise—an early birthday and Christmas present," he said, sliding an envelope over to me.

I opened the envelope and pulled out a card:

Pastry Making Class
Learn to Make Your Own Croissants
La Paris Cooking Classes
100 l'Hôtel de Ville
Paris, France

I could feel my mouth drop open, and I shouted, "No way! For real?"

Gong Gong smiled. "For real. You have to use it within a year because it expires. Don't let it expire."

"But how, Gong Gong? We can't afford to go to France!"

"Don't worry; remember, I used to work for Pan Am. I can still get a deal on plane tickets because I'm Gong Gong—they know me."

I grinned. "Yes, Gong Gong, everyone knows you. More importantly, does Mom know you got me this incredible gift?"

Immediately Gong Gong started shaking his head back and forth. "Ugh. Well, you know your mother. Just like your Aunt Krissy. Once someone plans something, then they have to invite everyone in the whole world so it's a party. They get that from your PoPo. The whole family is going, but don't worry—I am sure even you, Ruby, will have plenty of pastries all to yourself."

I was bubbling over just thinking about all the French food and pastries. "Oh, Gong Gong, you know me too well! I am going to eat so many French pastries you'll have to roll me home on my side like a vanilla macaron. Or maybe a chocolate macaron. I don't have a favorite macaron. I will have to taste test all of them and decide. Thanks, Gong Gong, for my gift! I can't wait to explore Paris with you. I already know I want to visit Angelina's and the Louvre Museum! There will be endless places to tour and eat!"

"This Angelina . . . how is her lemon tart? They have lemon tarts in France, right?" Gong Gong asked.

"Yes, Gong Gong, of course—we'll find the best *tarte au citron* in all of Paris," I said.

We grinned at each other, and I pulled out my phone to start investigating. The Fantastic Foo was back on the case and ready to jet across the world, again!